the Dublin Review

number eighty-two | SPRING 2021

GW00401075

EDITOR & PUBLISHER: BRENDAN BARRINGTON
DEPUTY PUBLISHERS: DEANNA ORTIZ & AINGEALA FLANNERY

The Dublin Review, number eighty-two (Spring 2021).
Design by Atelier David Smith. Printed by Naas Printing Ltd.

ISBN 978-1-9161337-6-1

SUBMISSIONS: Please go to www.thedublinreview.com and follow the instructions on the 'Submissions' page. Although we encourage electronic submissions, we also accept physical submissions, to The Dublin Review, P.O. Box 7948, Dublin 1, Ireland. We cannot return physical manuscripts, so please do not send a unique or irreplaceable piece of work, and be sure to include your email address for a reply. *The Dublin Review* assumes no responsibility for unsolicited material.

SUBSCRIPTIONS: *The Dublin Review* is published quarterly. A subscription costs €34 / UK£26 per year in Ireland & Northern Ireland, €45 / UK£36 / US$60 per year for the rest of the world. Institutions add €15 / UK£13 / US$20. To subscribe or to order back issues, please use the secure-ordering facility at www.thedublinreview.com. Alternatively, you may send your address and a cheque or Visa/MC data and order details to Subscriptions, The Dublin Review, P.O. Box 7948, Dublin 1, Ireland. Credit-card orders are billed at the euro price. Please indicate if credit-card billing address differs from mailing address. If you have a question regarding an order, please email us at order@thedublinreview.com.

WEBSITE: www.thedublinreview.com

TRADE SALES: *The Dublin Review* is distributed to the trade by Gill & Macmillan Distribution, Hume Avenue, Park West, Dublin 12.

SALES REPRESENTATION: Robert Towers, 2 The Crescent, Monkstown, Co. Dublin, tel +353 1 2806532, fax +353 1 2806020.

The Dublin Review receives financial assistance from the Arts Council.

Contents | *number eighty-two* | SPRING 2021

A posthumous existence

DAVID RALPH

On the night in question, when Zoe was still my fiancée, the four of us went clubbing, then ended sprawled on the floor around a low-slung table in the living room of Frank and Monika's apartment. My first vivid memory of the scene that ensued is of Frank saying 'How about we powder our noses again?' and tipping out another mound of the cocaine he'd produced once we'd got indoors.

'If you're going to get wet,' Zoe said, 'you might as well go swimming.'

Zoe had met Monika some months before at a yoga class, and we'd all become friendly. This was our first time at their place, which was large and open-plan and had the feel of a show apartment. There was an upright tree trunk with outstretched boughs fixed to a large marble base by the entrance, Japanese prints on the walls, and a carved African mask hanging out in the corridor. And, in the living room, a slate-framed photo of a scorched, forlorn landscape hung over the mantel. It put me in mind of a still from a Tarkovsky film.

I had my back to the window that ran from the floorboards to the high ceiling. Now and then I'd turn away from the room to stare through the windowpane and out across the square. We were all Dubliners, except Frank. He was from down the country someplace, Tipperary I think it was, though he didn't have the accent. He was in advertising, a senior creative, and he tended to dominate the talk.

'That's the spirit, Zoe,' he said.

'This is definitely the last one,' Monika said, sitting up. She rolled tight the banknote we'd been passing around. 'I'm so high.'

'Come on!' Frank said, chopping out lines with someone's credit card.

'When did we last do this?' He snatched the note from her.

Monika, picking at the cuticle of her pinkie, threw Frank a concerned look.

'Great view you have here,' I said, possibly not for the first time. We were six, seven storeys up, and the city swept away like a blurry meadow of glinting lights. There were cranes everywhere along the skyline again. 'We'll have to get you over to ours soon.'

Frank ignored this, picked up a different thread. 'I have three, maybe four friends who've children. And they've only two at most.' He ran a hand through his lacquered, jet-black hair. 'So out of – what? A hundred-odd friends, acquaintances.' He rubbed the residue of the line into his gums. 'That's eight kids, max.' He looked round the table, eyes all lit up. 'And I bet you're the same.'

'Basically,' I said. I stared out the window again. It was summer, and the city was bathed now in faint early-morning light. I thought I could make out the terraced house that we lived in then, behind the cathedral. 'The odd one has a kid,' I turned back to the room, 'but I suspect it's more of a lifestyle accessory with them.'

'Yeah!' Frank said. 'Degree – check! Job – check! Mortgage on the semi-d – check!' He made tick-marks in the air. 'And then the big one – a baby! But if you go a generation back, take a hundred adults. Fifty couples. Four kids apiece, minimum – that's two hundred kids screaming round the place.'

Monika picked up the note and, after seeming to hesitate, dropped her head towards the table. The parting at the side of her cropped, platinum-rinsed hair was at an oblique angle. Monika was petite and very pretty with big wonder-filled eyes. She was involved in some long-running saga with a doctorate in literary criticism.

'And what about you two?' Frank said. His nostrils flared. 'No notions?'

Zoe said, 'Notions!' Her lips were staining a deep red from the wine we were drinking. 'Aren't we *full* of notions?'

Zoe had followed her father into the law. He was once a junior minister in the government. My own father, after meeting Zoe for the first time, jokingly congratulated me for finding myself a 'laying hen'.

'Back to the issue,' he looked at us. 'What we're talking about here. Kids, children.'

'Oh God.' Zoe shrugged. 'You'd have to ask Nick that.' She reached across the table for the note, brushed a tendril of her thick auburn hair behind an ear. Even drunk and high, her movements were so exact, so elegant, like this was something we did all the time. 'Though I might need a rhinoplasty after tonight.'

'And I'll start saving for a vasectomy,' I said, taking the note from her. Zoe and I had never properly discussed our plans around children. I'd assumed we'd end up having one sooner or later, the way I imagined most couples just sort of fell into parenthood. 'Species extinction, here we come!'

'Exactly my point,' Frank said. 'My ex, Valerie, when we finally broke up – what'd she do? Immediately marries this ancient guy in his sixties! So that was her done, another genetic cul-de-sac.'

'You never told me this before,' Monika said. Her back was very straight now. 'But what's your point, love?'

'My point – there's plenty I've never told you before, pet. My point is our whole ...' Frank stopped talking. His attention had fixed on Zoe now. He leaned over the table, narrowed his eyes to a squint. 'Those are freshwater pearls, your earrings.'

'They are. How'd you know?'

'They're lovely.' He touched a hand to Zoe's ear. 'My mother used to grow them. And that spray of freckles across your nose. You're a lucky bastard, Nicky, you know that?'

We all laughed, as if the remark was much funnier than it was. But I knew Frank was speaking the truth. I had been kissed by good fortune in finding Zoe. We'd met at the ceremony of a short-film competition I'd won some years back. Ever since, Zoe had been supportive of my efforts to be a serious filmmaker, and by some miracle didn't seem overly concerned that I'd spent the subsequent years squandering various producers' money on one misconceived project after another.

'Oh Frank don't I know it,' I said. And I pictured Zoe and myself waltzing home later through the deserted streets, arms linked, up the hill of Christ Church and under the arch, past the Iveagh Trust buildings, before finally climbing those rickety old stairs to that big double bed we shared, in the house we rented off Zoe's parents at well below market rate.

I reached an arm round Zoe's ribs then.

'Go on, Nick,' she jutted her chin at the table. She gave my hand a quick squeeze and brushed it off. 'That stuff won't snort itself.'

The problem lay with what happened once Zoe and myself slipped into that big bed – or, more precisely, what didn't happen. I was beginning to wonder if what I'd assumed to be a mere phase wasn't something altogether more serious. But right now I felt good. I was glad I'd answered Frank's call earlier. We were having a fun time.

'And what about you guys?' I said once Frank had sat back down after changing the music to something that again I didn't recognize.

'What do you mean?' Frank said. His tone was aggressive. I noticed that.

'*Kids!* What we're talking about here.'

'Oh! Now *that's* below the belt, Nick.' Frank glanced from Zoe to Monika. 'Like asking how much money someone earns.'

Frank had a strong athletic build. We'd played squash together a few times. Seeing him naked in the locker room, I had the impression he used sunbeds. Afterwards we'd go for drinks and, as he flirted with the barmaids, he sometimes made noises about getting me in on ad shoots he was overseeing. I felt he was mocking me slightly, but that might have been my own paranoia.

'One sec,' Monika said, brushing away something from Frank's nose. Frank made a circle of her wrist with his hand, kissed her forehead. Then he had a drink of his wine.

'But aren't you keen to add your genes to the human cesspit?' I said.

'You did bring it up,' Zoe turned her smile on Frank, knocked a knee against his. 'Would you really deprive the world of your unique double-helix, Frank?'

Monika said, 'Frank thinks the world is *pullulating*.' She stroked his hair. 'Don't you, love?'

'And it's a shame because they'd be knockouts in the looks department,' and he fastened Monika's waist tight to him. 'Purebreds!'

'Well, I might be barren after tonight anyway,' Monika said, indicating the cocaine. 'God knows what's in that.' She reached out of Frank's clasp, refilled our glasses.

Zoe said, 'My company actually offers egg freezing as part of our salary package now.' This was news to me.

'They really are beautiful earrings,' Monika said. 'Hey! Frank, have you told Nick and Zoe about your mother's dating advice?'

'That old story.'

'It's great,' Monika said to us.

'I'm curious now,' I said.

'Christ! Since I have an audience,' Frank said. 'So, my mother was this very unassuming woman. But one time she was absolutely insistent with me. I'd finished school, had a summer job in a hotel up here. She's doused me in this snot-green holy water. "Now Francis, you're always to *ask*." And, you know, this is not a conversation I want to be having with my mother. But she has a grip of me. She says, "No, Francis, listen. You're always to ask."'

'Ask what?' Zoe said.

'Wait for this,' Monika said.

'Again she repeats her warning.'

'*What*, Frank?' I said.

'It's the small matter of my old man, Nick. He was never around. I think I told you that. I never actually met the man. But my mother's worried I mightn't be his only little misbegotten, you know. So she pulls me in tight again. "Francis," she goes, "girls you meet out – it could be a *sister* of yours."'

'Oh God!' Zoe said, covering her face with her hands.

'Yeah,' Frank said. 'She's petrified I'll have an incestuous affair with some halfling of mine!'

'Should have heard his chat-up lines,' Monika said.

And once more we all laughed.

I said to Frank, 'So you asked after Monika's stock then?'

'Nick, I had her do a fucking DNA test,' and he swabbed the inside of his cheek with a finger, snapping it out with a pop.

'Well. To always asking,' I said, and I thought that would be the end of it.

Frank heaped out a particularly large mound of cocaine this time and said, 'A child could easily fall out a window up here.'

'What are you on about, Frank?' I said. My lids were fluttering now, my face felt like it was pulling out of shape.

He cleared his throat, seemed about to say something. But he didn't. He turned his attention to the table, cut out more lines.

'You do much of this?' I said.

'Just special occasions.' He looked up at me. 'Like tonight.'

'It's pretty good,' and I ran my palms down my face again. I'd done my fair share after my film swept up all the newcomer awards.

The note was passed around again. I considered declining but didn't. It was a big fat slug that seared my nostril as it sailed up.

Then everyone seemed to start talking at once. Monika had her phone out showing us selfies she'd snapped earlier of us all twerking in the club. Zoe was rummaging in the depths of her shoulder-bag for tickets she'd gotten us to the Roderic O'Conor exhibition the next day and wondering if we should still try to make it. And Frank was going on about India having the fastest-expanding middle class in the world and how the market there for Irish whiskey was potentially huge if he just got the heritage story right on a …

I picked myself up, paced the room. I was alert and jumpy all of a sudden. I inhaled deeply, my heart thumping. I studied the Tarkovsky-ish photo over the mantel, but quickly I had to turn away from the desolate no-man's-land depicted there. Lately, I'd started waking in sweat-slicked terrors from a recurring dream in which my early-career acclaim kept being discussed in some magazine beneath a 'Whatever Happened To …' headline.

I went down the corridor to the bathroom, tried to steady myself in the mirror. I splashed water on my face, gripped the sink, closed my eyes for a while.

'You've been gone a long time' – Zoe's voice. Her lovely ovaline face was in the mirror when I opened my eyes. She threaded her arms through mine and around my waist.

'Have I?' I cupped my hands round her perfect haunches, slipped them inside the band of her skirt.

'Don't.'

I could feel the heat pulsing from her body through me. I pressed her in tighter.

'Stop, Nick.' There was a frost in her tone. 'Not here.' She dropped her arms from me. 'Frank's going a bit Tony Montana with the cocaine.'

'Ha! *Scarface*. Is it four years or five now since my BAFTA nomination?'

After a pause she said, 'Is it always going to be like this?'

'That's an excellent question.' I turned round to face her. 'One I've been wondering about myself.'

Zoe emitted a sort of sinking sound, her eyes rolled, then she walked out of the bathroom without another word.

*

Frank was standing against the windowpane and staring out across the square when I returned.

'Imagine the view once you're in the penthouse,' I said. I sat back down on the floor.

His shoulders rose and fell, he tilted his head. 'So I can look down on *every* cunt then,' he said in a loud voice.

The music must have stopped at a certain point. I could now hear the static of the turntable ticking past the needle as a new silence developed.

Monika glanced from Zoe to me.

'Have you heard the latest?' Frank said at last.

'What's that?' I said.

Frank turned back to the room, drained his glass. 'Monika is training to be a yoga guru.'

'*Teacher!* Yoga *teacher*, Frank.'

He came over to the table, swept up a bottle by the neck, drained that too. 'And you think you've heard it all.' Then he crossed the room and tossed the bottle into a corner, calling out as he went down the corridor, 'Another dead soldier!'

Somehow, the bottle didn't smash.

Over at the kitchen island I made a great production of opening more wine, groaning and huffing when the cork got stuck. My eye again caught the slate-framed photo as I came back to the table with fresh drinks for everyone.

'Really! You'd be a great yoga teacher,' Zoe was saying.

'Well, Frank is abroad so much with work,' Monika said. 'And the space here could easily be converted to a studio.'

'Light a few votive candles,' I said. 'Incense.'

'For one-to-one lessons,' Monika added.

'Brilliant idea!' Zoe said, and I knew she was lying. Her views were closer to Frank's on this.

'Here, let's do some more coke,' I sighed deeply. 'We'll all be levitating soon.'

I scratched out more lines. The women went first.

'Hey! That photo,' I nodded at the mantel, sniffling. 'It's from some movie, right?'

'Must be Frank's,' Monika said. 'Was here when I moved in. Probably from some ad he did.'

'What's Frank's?' I heard Frank say. He was back in the doorway.

'That photo,' I said. 'I recognize it from some movie.'

'You're mistaken, Nick.'

Then he went over to the window, pressed his face to the windowpane.

'Frankie,' Monika said, her voice pleading, 'sit down.'

'Though it could be from a script for one,' Frank sneered.

'Why don't you sit down, love?' Monika patted the floor.

'What's it from then?' I said.

'It'll be morning soon,' Frank said.

'There's a line for you here, Frank,' I said. 'And a drink.'

'As you said, Nick, a fine view. South-facing aspect.' He balled his hands to fists. 'I like you, Nick. I fucking like you.'

'And I you, Frank.'

'We could go for breakfast soon,' Zoe said cheerily. To my relief, it sounded like she was over her hump. 'Hit up an early-house.'

'Great idea!' Monika said. 'Hey! Frankie, there's this new place we haven't tried yet, remember?'

'New, old – same bullshit.' He still had his back to us. 'You know where that photo's from, Nick?' He had relaxed his hands again.

A flare streaked through the sky, or so I thought. 'Is it *Stalker*?'

'They serve shark there,' Monika said quickly. 'Shark!'

'Reminds me of the Zone in *Stalker*,' I said.

Frank turned round to face us. 'No, Nick, it's not from any movie, I said.'

'Or is it *The Sacrifice*?'

'*Nick*, it's not from any *fucking* film,' Zoe said. 'Would you let Frank tell his story?'

'My mother was so lucid right up to the end, Nick,' he said. 'Despite all the drugs they'd her on. There was this one story she never got –'

'Love, you've told us this already,' Monika said. 'Remember? Always ask,' and she looked to us as if for support.

'Would you please be quiet, Monika,' Frank said then in a low voice. 'Do me that small favour. I'm trying to tell Nicky something.'

Frank put his nose through the line, then went to the mantel and removed the slate-framed photo from the wall.

'So my mother,' he said after placing the photo on the table and sitting down beside us. 'She wasn't too far off with her warnings. Turns out, there is a half-sister after all!'

'You've a half-sister!' Monika said.

'Laura's her name.'

'Why didn't you tell me before?' Monika said in a wounded voice.

'Laura McGrath. I'm telling you now. Would you like her number?'

'How did this all happen, Frank?' Zoe said.

'I get this email,' Frank looked round the table. 'All the usual clichés, would I be up for meeting. So we meet. She tells me about the old man. Turns out they lived just over the border in Limerick. He was a "writer", managed one pathetic novel, sum of his life's work. His father was a tyrant, I'm told by way of clarification or justification, or something. But – here's the thing. After he died, Laura's mother tells her about *me*. She's never mentioned it before, wants to come clean. Laura's shocked to learn she has this half-brother. But the reason Laura contacts me, it's something the old man said before they were married. Now Laura's mother has died suddenly, and she's feeling some pangs of I-don't-know-what. That's when she emails.'

'And how'd the meeting go, Frank?' Zoe again.

'So the thing Laura wants to tell me. It's a few months before the old man's wedding. I'm maybe four, five by then. He has a sister – I guess she'd be my *aunt*, right? It turns out this *aunt* was sort of friendly with my mother. I mean, my *mother* was with him for a few years. Anyway. This aunt asks him if he's ever told his fiancée about the child he has with another woman. This woman who is not exactly a million miles away. No, he hasn't, he says. You have to tell her before the wedding, she says. It's not fair she doesn't know. I will, I will, he promises. A few weeks go by. The wedding preparations are moving along. Church is booked, reception organized. The aunt corners him a second time. Well? she goes. Well what? he goes. You know what, she goes. Do I have to do this myself? He rears up – no no no, I'll sort this out. The aunt warns him again: if he doesn't tell the fiancée, she will. Basic decency he tell his wife-to-be about me. A few more weeks go by. The big day is very close now. It's the dress rehearsal in the church. A third time the aunt confronts him. I'm going up to that altar this minute and telling her, she tells him. Imagine the scene! OK OK, he tries to calm her. He says, I'll tell her straight after the rehearsal.'

'So he told her then?' Zoe said in a tremulous voice, as if she couldn't quite believe what she was hearing.

'Yes and no. He gets her away from the church, away from the aunt. Goes for a drive, pulls in somewhere quiet. Says to his fiancée, "I have something to tell you. Something about my past."'

There was a silence, during which I grew certain this was Frank's first time ever telling anyone this story. He was looking about the room. He took a long swig of his drink. For once it seemed he might be stuck for words.

'And what did he say then, Frank?' It was Zoe who said this, who broke the silence.

A wry grin warped his handsome features as he considered the photo. 'When his fiancée asks where the baby is now he turns to her and says,

"Sadly the baby boy died in infancy."'

'Jesus Christ!' Zoe said and lifted a hand to her mouth.

'You said it, Zoe,' and he laughed here. Then Frank glared at Monika and said, 'All of this, it's all my posthumous existence. Do you get it *now*?'

And that was when Monika picked herself off the floor and walked out of the room.

I jerked my head at Zoe, to indicate she should follow Monika. She just stared back dead-eyed at me. Then she topped up our glasses.

'And Frank,' she said, casting him a searching look, 'what did you do after hearing that?

'Well. This Laura tells me something else in passing. His house – it's vacant. She's trying to sell it. She's moved off years ago, married, all that. So I make a few phone calls, let on I'm a city boy looking for a rustic holidaying spot. A year passes. Eventually it's up on the market. There's minimal interest. I have an agent do my bidding.'

'So you own his house?' Zoe said.

'You might say that. After the sale I had a demolition team lined up within a week. Had them tear the place down.'

'You're kidding, Frank?' I said.

'Even the dog-shed, Nick. Razed. To the fucking ground. And once every last brick and slate and cable was removed I had the earth ploughed up too. The roots of the cypress trees in the garden I had ripped out, torched.' Frank stood up abruptly, jerked a thumb at the photo. 'I walked away after that, let nature do its worst.'

We just sat there staring up at him.

'Right folks,' he called out crossing the floor, 'Frank's finished,' and he disappeared down the corridor.

Zoe surprised me by racking up two more lines. Big ones. She came up from the table sucking hard at the air.

'What'd you make of all that?' I said as I took my turn at the table.

'Of all what?'

I tried to keep my voice down. 'All that stuff about Frank's father. Crazy, no?'

Zoe shook her head, let out this mirthless laugh.

'What?'

'Nick,' she said in a low voice. She poured us more wine.

'Well, at least we learned why Frank's so anti-children,' and I laughed at this.

'Is that what you learned?'

'It's pretty obvious, no? The whole destruction of the temple,' and I pointed to the photo.

The way her gaze was fixed on me now was starting to unnerve me.

'Am I missing something?'

'He doesn't think he's fit to be a father. At least he's honest with himself, Nick.'

'Fit to father? Is that a legal category?'

She hugged her knees tight to her chin. She worried her lower lip with an incisor. She was shaking her head again.

I went to the window and stared out. The light was very painterly then, I remember, this sort of powder blue. A single star still burned in the sky. A work van rolled into the square below. A cat stalked across the cobbles.

'*Nick!*' she called.

'Zoe,' I said. But I didn't face her.

'Look, Nick. I should've told you this sooner …'

Through the tangle of cranes squiggling the skyline I was searching for our little house behind the cathedral.

Zoe's voice was solid in the air. She was talking about her father. Her father was selling the house. There was the market to consider. Zoe talked on. At a certain point I heard her saying she might move home for a while. At a later point I heard her asking me if I understood what she meant.

I don't recall if I nodded my head or spoke aloud.

In the silence I continued scanning the rooftops.

I knew I'd have to turn back to the room eventually. But for the longest time I kept standing there, staring out, unable to find our little house behind the cathedral.

A critic at large

MAGGIE ARMSTRONG

Adventure time. I had my fill.

I was young, I liked to think, and V, let's call him, produced the best holidays from his imagination. Sudden trips: chateaux, rectories, hunting lodges, revamped lighthouses, abandoned coastguard stations – he got the last-minute deals and haggled them down, swept us off, lost no time, insisted on constant diversion. And although there were bad roads taken, missed flights and funks and crack-ups, we always came home invigorated, flattened, with stories to tell.

V loved the States, and I had never been before. 'Everything is just so big, so outsized and disgraceful!' he'd say, waving hands. It was summer, and he wanted to go for a whole month. I had a bit of money saved from my publishing job and my recently axed restaurant column, and he had wads of cash – from what? That took a while to figure out.

At Dublin Airport, a woman told us we had missed our flight. 'It's gone. Plane's gone – you're two hours late.' We could try for standby seats tomorrow, or fly from Shannon on Wednesday? For the shortest second I thought this was a sign: it was not meant to be. But V didn't think like that; the missed flight made him reckless and creative. At a bus stop, with our bags in the rain, he reported what was happening. 'Torrential, absolutely heartbreaking, but probably the challenge that makes us, gorgeous, so then, let's get some seaside in, let's minimize our misery here, gorgeousness.' The luscious pet names had a sedative effect on me, I was very much in love.

The bus took us to an empty fishing village where, over mugs of beer and scampi fries, I opened a tabloid newspaper looking for an article I had written: my last restaurant column. Sitting there, I was so absorbed in my own sentences I didn't notice he'd gone quiet and jerky, how his face was pale and clenched.

'Right, you're not listening. Oh you are? What did I just say then?' V pushed his chair away from the table and left the little bar. I wondered, looking at a desolate Dublin shoreline, how it was going to be possible to continue this holiday. Moments later I was running after him on the flinty grey beach, in the swampy rain, lunging over rockpools, begging him to understand. Everyone deserves a holiday.

The next morning, we failed again. 'The standby seats are not available, no,' said another woman, this time with laughter in her eyes. The only option was Shannon. We got on a bus to Limerick, and found a room in a large hotel where I crawled up to his face and breathed, 'You know I am so excited to be here with you.'

In the taxi from JFK I gazed at the line of skyscrapers and tried to form original impressions. What's so special about going anywhere, when everything looks so much better in pictures anyway? Why am I so upset on holiday, why am I so ungrateful, so abnormal?

The hotel was big and brash and in-your-face, but he'd had a good time there with one of his ex-wives, and I was easy. At reception the lady looked confused.

'Sir, it was a no-show, we were obliged to give up your room.'

'We called,' he told this tall, calm, sympathetic Black woman. 'Didn't we, gorgeous? You all seem very confused. This is a major booking we are talking about, you will have to make this right again. I'll stand here until you ...' Eventually another woman came to say that she was so sorry, the hotel was taking care of this. After that they upgraded us to a triple king deluxe room with park views.

There was a giant bed with a soft pink bedspread that licked the room like a frothing tongue. Waiting on a table were two purple orchids, two flutes of champagne and two brownies, glazed with chocolate sauce and decorated with a pair of American flags on cocktail sticks. We were on the sixth floor, overlooking the trees of Central Park. V beheld the view with outstretched arms and cracked his back, which ached from travel. I tore off my clothes, picked a cocktail stick out of a brownie, sucked the chocolate off and took a long sip of the plonk.

In the morning, soft from the shower, I felt something pierce my heel. I screamed and rocked on the floor clutching my foot, then pulled out the cocktail stick by its miniature star-spangled banner.

We went to Central Park, where V ran and I panted after him in my thrift-store frock and love-heart sunglasses – 'Don't lag, don't embarrass yourself now,' he blared. I was desperately unfit and my foot still hurt, but V had adrenaline to expend. We went window shopping, to Bloomingdale's and Tiffany's. I walked around half-conscious in his protective shadow, always smiling at the air he breathed. He was handsome like an overgrown Hollywood star, with a sheepish air, a cruel sense of humour and unpredictable energy. Flamboyant hands. He wore, those days, a crushed linen suit jacket buttoned too tight, striped Brooks Brothers shirts, corduroys and bulky white unbranded tennis shoes. It was usually enough to merely stand there and exist, a relief to know this was personality enough for two.

We went to Williamsburg to visit a restaurant I'd read about in a magazine, but we couldn't find the right street and we were weak with jetlag. We walked for three hours under the burning sun, nodding at Puerto Rican men selling fruit or hardware. I limped, and on the side of the street V doused my heel with alcohol then put the bandage on wrong. When we found the restaurant, it looked worryingly small and decrepit, like a shack. We were seated on a terrace surrounded by plants, with twinkling lights. Next to us three very slim athletic people were talking about interiors over rosé and crostini. Everyone glanced at each other, up and down. They probably didn't take me for V's daughter – not quite – but I still liked the curiosity in their saucy eyes. Cocktails arrived, with elderflower and dandelion. I began to read the menu.

'Wow!' I said.

'Wow for you,' he said. 'What about me? There's nothing for me here.'

'Summer sausage with labneh and almonds?'

I scanned the menu again. Brick chicken, three types of oyster. Soppressata?

'What about oysters?' I hedged. 'Do you eat oysters?'

'Do I eat cunts?' he said and I knew that it was happening again. His face was very white and only his mouth moved. 'It's all about you, isn't it?' His head trembled very faintly and one eye popped out as he explained why it was we needed to leave.

We got up, apologized, and walked silently to Rick's Cheese Steak. That night, I slept on the sofa in the hotel room while V took the deluxe king-size bed.

We mostly ate in diners after that. Or we ate roast beef sandwiches on benches and the tall sliced meat toppled onto the ground in red piles to be plucked at by pigeons. Or we ate crisps. I got many takeaway Starbucks iced lattes with whipped cream and cinnamon sugar on top, and paraded them through the streets, like candy floss for adults. My foot oozed a little and every night I iced it back at the hotel, or painted my fungal toenail with a medical varnish while V switched news channels, crushed newspapers in outstretched arms, played with his phone, catnapped, made relaxed phone calls, finally waiting at the door for me – come on, let's get out of here, Manhattan's waiting, life's short.

He said I should see Ellis Island and the Statue of Liberty and booked a special tour boat around Manhattan Island. Seated with the tour group, I wrote the day's date on a fresh blank page. I'd bought a Kate Spade notebook from a Macy's display and I planned to write down everything we saw. Now I wondered what to eat for lunch. I thought, There's the Statue of Liberty, and look, I have nothing to say.

The tour began. V couldn't hear the tour guide over the boat's engine. 'Can you hear anything?' he asked me. 'Can any of you hear anything?' he asked the people sitting behind us.

'Not so much,' said an agreeable tourist, maybe Dutch.

'Swindle,' he said. 'We are playing thirty dollars each, that's sixty I've dropped.' He fidgeted and thrashed in his seat. He went to the man with the microphone, then teetered back towards me.

'Full volume, not good enough I'm afraid. This is – hey –' to the calm Dutch tourist and others in the plastic seats around – 'Hey, can you hear that guy? Can you hear that guy? Yeah, it's annoying, right? You know, there's enough of us to do something about this.'

'Mutiny?' suggested the agreeable Dutch tourist, smiling.

'He's not serious,' I said, but he was gone again, now leaning gigantically into the guide.

He marched back. 'We can get a group of us together, let's not stand for it,' he said, and I gazed out to sea, imagined being inside the icy waves. I burned and froze at once, looked down, touched my sandalled foot with its peeling, filth-gathering bandage – it could be now, I thought, no time like now.

We found ourselves standing next to the Metropolitan Museum of Art, so we went in, laughing. One of the guards asked V not to lean against a wall. 'Says who? I can lean against a publicly provided wall.' The guard, suddenly nervous, requested we make our way out since the museum was closing anyway. 'Sir, move along,' said the guard, and V said, 'Where is the sign? You're saying we can't look at these things?' 'Move along, sir,' the guard said. 'Hold on now,' said V as my internal organs shrivelled. 'What time is closing? Seven p.m. – we have thirty minutes. We can look at artefacts until seven p.m., we paid for all this, we paid for this little, this little clay pipe or this little pestle or this nice little tool, this spear, out of our pocket, I'm just looking at this nice little primitive spear. These are ancient things belonging to the people, not your personal fossil collection, my girlfriend and I would like to take a good look at this probably violently seized loot, we are on holidays!!!' And he walked slowly, crablike, through the great hallway, his eyes pinned on the glass boxes, glancing at me to share the joke, breathing quickly, brows arched, and the flashing eyeball.

All the way back to the hotel, we shouted. None of these people will ever see us again, I told myself. In the room, I iced my heel and we shouted, V at the foot of the bed stretching his hamstrings in an impromptu warm-up with his head lancing back and forth. We watched CNN, then dinner was pro-posed. We got dressed up.

In my restaurant reviews, I would write philosophically about eating out. I would argue that you could be happy in a restaurant whatever your state of mind, because of the time-honoured contract: knowing that these artisans will restore you with fortifying dishes as you shower the place with your precious earnings and best self. Together, we the citizens of the earth will brave each other and be alive and well. We will sit up straight and use cut-lery and watch the subtle theatre loosen and unwind, all of us flawed and equal, and wine will pour through our veins making talk light and fun.

The hotel bar had a bland modern feel, phenomenal prices.

'Hamburger,' he said.

I took out my notebook and wrote down his order. I still thought of myself as a restaurant critic, I suppose, and intended to document every-thing. V asked what I was doing and then pulled back his chair. 'Right,' he said. 'Right then.'

We sat at a distance, boiling rapidly under our skins. I was stunned – I was still capable of being stunned – by how quickly things could turn bad. We fought in our seats, with gimlet eyes, at a rising pitch.

'Everyone is looking at us!' I said.

Food came, a robbery on plates. Women with facelifts, dangling martini glasses, appeared disturbed at the sight of us. A woman near us called over a waiter and changed tables.

I can go, I thought, waking later that night to see him lurch through the bedroom making animal sounds – I can pack up and go. This can end here.

'I'm sorry it didn't work out,' I said the next morning, pulling my suitcase out the door while he got dressed. And I sat in the dim-lit WiFi zone by the reception of a hotel that to this day sends me promotional emails. I sat on my suitcase, insufferable chill-out music in my ears. We were due to check out that morning either way, find somewhere cheaper. I had a cousin on the Upper West Side. I wrote her an email, edited the email, and didn't send it. There was no explaining what had happened, certainly not to someone else, and to invent something would be a sad affair: I was not a liar. I also wished now that it hadn't actually happened. So I took the elevator back up again, right up to the sixth floor, went down the corridor and opened the door with my carefully retained room card.

V was gone. Even the complimentary shampoos and shower gels were gone.

On the hot street, I stared into the froth of my Starbucks. I ate a fingerful of cream, then set off, wandering around Central Park. A stone sculpture of Alice in Wonderland sitting on a toadstool yielded up no answers. I hauled my suitcase into the subway and then around the Lower East Side. I bumped it up a stairway to try to bargain for a room that was unaccountably creepy – then changed my mind, and bumped it back down again, and sweated over to a hostel whose bedrooms were the size of toilet cubicles. I spent three nights in one of these sleep coffins, woken at eight every morning by a low smartphone alarm that sounded gently up the walls for an hour or more.

I wrote to V. 'It doesn't mean I don't miss you.'

He wrote back. 'I'm right here.'

We stood on Times Square, shocked by the lights and possibilities, consulted ticket prices, and walked away again. We trailed around Greenwich Village – I wanted to see a folk band, but he met a guy scalping tickets to Louis CK. 'Louis CK! He's huge! What an opportunity!' I said I didn't like stand-up comedy. It's not funny, I suggested, because every joke has been rehearsed so as to give people their money's worth. He said I just wasn't much fun, wasn't game. 'You're about as fun', he riffed, 'as the guy who absent-mindedly discards the banana skin that the funny guy slips on in the slapstick. As fun as the guy who gets the cream cake thrown on his face!' I sucked up the dregs of my Starbucks coffee, making a harsh hoovering sound with the straw. What I liked, at the end of the long days, was that he did the talking, the explaining, he made me laugh in unrepeatable ways, you really had to be there.

We rented bikes. Ate overpriced pastrami on rye from a famous deli. Lost the bikes and had to walk home. My heel stung where the toothpick wound had re-opened, and the pain each time I took a step seemed to surge up through my body, all the way to my left shoulder. His weight pounded me in the bed-sized hostel room and he murmured in my ear about what a privilege this was. I accepted the mistake we would now make. To rent a car, go south – a factored-in mistake, too grand a plan to dodge at this late stage. I didn't want to ever be boring. I wrote things down with a mind to one day tell stories, entertain, but only really wanted to be entertained, hypnotized.

Our final evening in New York City we sat on the floor of a crowded bus station with tired mothers, small children and babies who screamed. Something had gone wrong with the rental car V had booked – I can't remember what – and he objected to the price of booking a new one elsewhere at the last minute. The bus to Richmond departed at midnight and we slept not at all. In the waking city, we rented a room for a day, pulled the stiff sheets over our faces.

We got a car in Richmond. V took the driver's seat, adjusting every setting, too big for this world, and he turned the engine on. He smiled: 'Sure you can trust your tormenter?'

He normally did the driving. I was happier navigating. I used a Michelin Road Atlas of the USA, Canada and Mexico, drawing a line with a biro and always at pains to hold the map the right way. There was no particular route, or destination, other than an idea about the South, its lost romance. The car was bulky and unglamorous and he drove very fast looking at the fancy media screen, beating his finger on the news channels.

We ate at diners and waffle houses and pancake huts. On Virginia Beach, bobbing in the pale sea, he asked me to please not pass him the yeast infection from my genitals. In Colonial Williamsburg, having a beer, he told me I had the face of a prawn.

We drove and drove. We drove until my legs were giddy and his back got locked into painful positions. We drove and the grey life zoomed away from us in sheets upon sheets of road like a roll of grey tape unwound accidentally.

Late one night, we stopped at a motel advertising a swimming pool on a sign flashing red and yellow. We parked the car, walked up and pressed a buzzer. The curtain scraped open, and a shock went through me. A girl stood in a glass box a metre over us, teeth hanging from her mouth. Teeth splayed every which way, all different shades and textures – jagged, serrated, discoloured by death. Teeth from an internet picture, from a book of freaks. The girl was skinny, with big hoop earrings, and flowers painted on her long fake nails. A sign requested patrons to declare their weapons, and she nodded, chewing her chin as she welcomed us.

She led us past the grim line of apartments and the benighted swimming pool. What troubled me, as I lay down, was the thought that those teeth were the reason this girl was here, in the dead of night, letting armed strangers into an enclosure with her, while I rode free, and never had to put my life at risk. The girl was unlucky, V agreed, and we should not go close to her or something bad might happen to us, too. Or was it too late? I moved right next to him, shuddering – we really bonded over other people's hard luck.

'Can you ensure that nothing bad will happen?' I knew this was a stupid and naïve thing to say.

'Well no,' he said thoughtfully, stroking my hair. 'But I can assure you I'll always be there.'

Raleigh was a place I'd mythologized. There is a catchy song that mentions dying in Raleigh, though I had never looked into what this might mean. Our holiday was nearly over. The heel of my right foot throbbed. When I touched the bandage, I could feel how the wound still wept.

We found the restaurant I'd been aiming for. A blocky waiter with his shirt sleeves expertly rolled came to our table.

'It's nice to meet you both. What are your names? I'm Drew, and I'm going to be your server tonight, it's my third day, so you gotta go easy on me!'

'We're in heaven,' I said, ordering up a storm: Creole gumbo, plantation salad, blue cheese and spiced pecans. Fried green tomatoes, Louisiana crawfish. Boudin balls with pepper jelly and pickled okra. We ate with great appetite, licking the crumbs from our fingers and gulping back the day-expelling beer. Drew would come and say, 'All to your satisfaction, MA'AM?', and, 'WOULD YOU LIKE ANOTHER FROSTY BEER, MY MAN?' Food and drink kept on arriving. North Carolina catfish, fried oyster, gulf shrimp. Hush puppies, fries and slaw and remoulade. Hoop cheddar mac 'n' cheese.

Shrimp 'n' grits, and cornbread stuffed with – quail? Fritters.

I looked up. 'What's wrong?' I asked because he had gone white again. I was doing it again. Writing in my notebook, smiling, it was my deathly flaw – vanity, delinquent self-regard. The space between us became tense, almost material, and I got up and sat at a separate table, glancing up every so often to see the pin-cushion tops of his eyes. And when Drew came and produced the long curling bill, I threw down some notes and left the place on my own.

This was unforgivable.

'No, I've had enough!' I stamped my foot, the good one, then cast around for the street the car was on.

However, it was only ten o'clock at night. We were on holidays, and we both wanted the same things. An interesting time, young-person fun. We walked shouting, then looked up and saw a tacky club doing drinks promotions. Still shouting, but this time out of necessity because of the awful music, we exchanged a word about the drunk-driving laws – he'd had too much beer and now he was having two cocktails for one. Driving under the influence was disgusting, obviously, but V was good company, out on the town, and at that point I would have held on to anything good as compensation for such a shambles as this was. We got back in the car.

The roads were strikingly empty as we kept an eye out for a place to stay. We talked, first quietly, then quickly, about what had gone wrong at dinner, what kept going wrong and the damage this could cause, and he turned from the driver's seat and shouted, 'I know this world and I know how to get us out of this world yeah watch!' He stretched his body long, the car sped up, he accelerated so hard the road began to devour itself, the wheels lifted into gruesome nothingness.

You understand, sometimes, that what is happening is no nightmare or illusion. All precious things are out of your hands. His face was elsewhere and the car was now careening. I screamed at him to stop the car. Again and again I screamed. It is demeaning to have to be so hysterical when it comes to something as important as your life. 'You're trying to scare me!' – these words scattered.

There was the clear shape of a tree, then another tree. Objects moved past with their integrity, and not as sheets of whitish lines. We drove saying nothing, only breathing, until a box of light came up ahead. An enormous multi-storey hotel, and we turned inside and parked.

Everything was white, with every screen and light burning, a mammoth fuse waiting to blow, but it didn't. The world was so comfortingly impassive. We were safe. He went to bed as he was so tired from the driving. I sat in the monstrous lobby watching two TV screens play different channels side by side, and drank sweet hot chocolate from a sachet. I wished that I could be more miserable than I was.

'Had another fight with V,' I wrote in my notebook.

We stopped in ugly motels, in smoking rooms with fat wingèd bugs flying in the showers. We drove and drove and drove and drove and drove and he made sudden clamorous protestations about having to drive all day every day and so I would tenderly dig my thumbs into the hide of his neck, to release tension. Drove and drove and drove. He had a compulsion, the odd time, to stop the car and run through a wooded area to let everything out, all the madness – 'Here, now!' he'd say and he'd pull into a verge in some bleak spot, the daylight fading, and get out and sprint while I leaned on the bonnet and wondered about, god forbid, lunch, dinner? He would come back dripping with sweat and say, 'Sorry about that. But we have a nice time, don't we, gorgeous?'

There was the odd exhilarating old song on the radio and I would sing along with an almost unbearable sense of happiness. Or a Starbucks would glide by us and I'd say 'Stop!' And nestle into the seat with a plastic cup of whipped cream iced latte to gorge upon.

At one point, we decided for no specific reason but with urgent inspiration to get to Charleston by that evening. The drive took a whole day. We arrived near midnight, and found a sports bar open. My foot hurt, so I held it in my hand and hopped, then leaned on his shoulder. The barman carried two ice-cold pints on a round tray, and we tipped him. We ordered everything on the menu. Nachos. Balls of potato like the McCain potato smiles I ate with disappointment as a child. Hamburgers. We both came to life with beer. I agreed to dig my pincers into his neck, look for knots along his cliff-side back and work them out. We were delirious, walking to the car.

He started up the engine. He was over the limit, but so was I and he was bigger, and the Travelodge wasn't far. I held the map as he steered us up a wide, tree-lined avenue. 'Go left go left,' I said suddenly.

The impact came from my side. A giant thorn, an industrial wasp-sting. Assault of metal. Something wrong. We seemed to twist, and squeeze.

There was a car alarm piercing through the night. I wondered – dozy, as if waking from a deep sleep – if we would be very badly injured. We were pulled out of the car through the driver's side, lifted into the arms of – a policeman? And I was standing at the boot beside V, who was looking in suitcases for a chocolate bar that would take the alcohol out of our breaths. I was stuffing a row of mint chocolate squares in my mouth and he said in my ear, 'If anyone asks, you were driving.'

In the middle of the junction was a bright red sports car with the bonnet bashed in. The driver's seat was empty. I sat on the kerb, confused, while V walked around, taking witness statements using his voice-recording app. Two excited women were telling him how the other car had been going very fast. The driver had run away, left his licence, the fool.

They did not breathalyze us. I knew it was possible I had been holding the map sideways. The policeman drove us to our Travelodge, which was not at all where I had thought it was.

In bed that night, my heart banged. Somewhere down the road, a petrified boy racer was hiding in bushes. Or maybe they had found him already.

Had he turned up at the police station? Was he even out of school? Was he in tears this moment? I wondered would he cry more about his stupid car or about the way his life was turning out. Which meant I wondered was he someone worth sympathizing with.

If anyone asks, you were driving: What a bad man.

I woke up, the next morning and the ones that followed, realizing that I wished I had been physically injured. I wanted to be partially crushed.

The last stop was Washington, for the flights. Maybe we got there by bus. There was also a small airport. And there was another hired car, provided by the insurance company possibly, but the details are gone, forgotten. I was half conscious most of the time. We booked ourselves into an inn with carved bedposts and dainty curtains. I stared some time at the ceiling, then rolled sideways on the bed and took off my shoes and socks. I had to do something I had been putting off. Slowly, unbreathing, I unpeeled the dog-eared bandage and peeked under. Everything was nauseated, the room quivered. The back of the foot was sick and yellowish green and still swollen. V was gone running. I considered shutting my eyes and refusing to move until our flight. Instead I phoned reception.

There was a doctor on the hotel's emergency contacts list who was willing to see me, and he was just a couple of blocks away. The doctor opened his surgery door and said in a lilting way, like in an old film, 'Take off your shoes, lie down, what is your name?' and I wanted to melt into the foam bed of his care. This doctor picked around with silver instruments, and I bit my fist. He bent his knees, turning his head this way and that. The doctor went very quiet. He called a second person in, another doctor or a nurse, and she ran steaming water from the sink into a basin. 'May I?' The doctor then plunged my foot in the warm water. He picked around some more; I was worried as usual that I was about to die.

'It's gangrenous, you have to chop it off!' I said, and then the doctor, that burly medicine man, pulled from the hard mushroom flesh of my heel a shard of cocktail stick dyed with blood.

The doctor bandaged the hole in soft white gauze and neatly taped it, then wrote out a prescription for antibiotics and anti-inflammatories to which he added, in strong cursive, 'elevation and bed rest'. As we said goodbye I wanted to thank him from the bottom of my heart – I wanted to see him again, this doctor, and even marry him.

I lay dazed in the quaintly furnished inn, another establishment still intent on drawing me back with promotional emails. 'Wound got infected,' I said, and V sat up next to me on the pillows.

'Infected? *Infected*? Awful. Horrible. My poor sweetheart. You have suffered, you deserved none of this. I'm taking you out, I want us to have one good memory.'

We chose a high-end Italian delicatessen in pleasant Georgetown and it was spectacular, the hanging hams, everything, but he didn't like a cheese that I did, so we ended up sitting at different tables some distance apart, exchanging sour looks. We ate opposing Black Forest gateaux, and he sent the bill to my table.

Reset

JESSICA TRAYNOR

When my daughter was first placed on my chest, gasping and blood-smeared, my immediate feeling was pity as she stared at me with flat, black eyes. Neither of us had asked for this frightening birth.

Then she was whipped away from me.

1

The previous morning – my due date – I'd stepped out of the shower to find some water on the floor. Had I splashed it out of the shower? It was a tiny amount – nothing like the torrent that signifies the dramatic beginnings of labour in movies. I dried myself off and waited. Nothing happened – no leaking, no contractions. I got dressed and went downstairs, where I made myself a cheese sandwich and sat on the sofa with my phone. I had been told first babies never arrive on their due date. All the mothers I'd met at pregnancy yoga had dark tales of two-week waits and inductions. Inductions were what you wanted to avoid. They were painful, unnatural, traumatic.

I didn't ask why, because I didn't want to know.

My relatives had had trouble with childbirth. I was unclear on the medical details, but there seemed to be an issue with big babies vs. small cervixes. One second cousin was left with a permanently damaged arm because of a botched forceps birth.

Coming up to my due date, I'd had weekly visits with the midwives in the hospital for blood tests. I have a low platelet count, which can lead to uncontrolled bleeding. Thinking about the subject made me picture Lionel

Barrymore as wild-eyed Rasputin in the 1932 film *Rasputin and the Emperor* coaxing the hypnotized, haemophiliac Prince Alexei from his bed: a scene that had filled me with dread when I'd seen it as a child. I didn't ask for details about uncontrolled bleeding, but as my bump got bigger and my visits to the hospital more regular, I sometimes asked one of the revolving circle of friendly midwives: *Is this baby too big? Is there any way we can check? Do I need to be prepared for a C section?*

The response: 'Do you *want* a C section?'

'No, I'd just like to avoid an emergency one.'

A tape measure would be whipped out, one end applied to my clavicle and the other to my groin. The midwife would smile. 'The baby is a perfectly healthy size.'

The weeks before the due date were a strange time. Living close to my workplace in Dublin's north inner city, I walked everywhere. My frustration at having become a slow-moving galleon was intense. As the weeks went by, and my walking pace got slower and slower, a different streetscape emerged. I found myself existing in the time-stream of the elderly and the vulnerable. Drug addicts nodding on the edge of the kerb, swaying in a non-existent breeze, or scuffling themselves along with their feet in hospital-issue wheelchairs. Old ladies pushing their trolleys doggedly in the direction of FX Buckley's, where they'd suck their dentures while waiting for their small weekly pickings: a few sausages, some orange-seasoned chicken if they were feeling exotic. The tripe that my granny used to boil for my granddad in milk, leaving an abattoir stench in their house.

On a bright clear day in September a strange man stopped me as I was passing FX Buckley's on my way to the Rotunda for a check-up. I assumed he was asking directions, but before I could react, he had placed his hand on my lower back. 'When you go into labour, the pain will be here,' he said. His face had a strange zealous gleam, Rasputin's staring eyes. I stood rooted in horror and indignation at this touching.

I moved away. 'OK. Thank you.'

He subtly shifted his position on the pavement so he was standing in my path. 'They all think the pain will be in the front, but looking at you, it'll be in the back. But you'll be fine,' he said, 'you won't need drugs. It's a pain you're prepared for. It's a pain *all* women are prepared for.'

'OK. I have to go.'

He tried to grasp my hand and, when I flinched back, settled for a strange little priesteen-bow, palms together. I tried to accelerate around him, but my heft wouldn't let me build up speed. The skin on my back crawled until I'd rounded the corner. I couldn't wait to leave this strange, slow world where I was unable to sprint away from danger, this world that seems reserved for those about to cross the Styx.

I wanted my body back.

2

Often during the pregnancy I was seized by the worry that I had made a mistake. I had never been broody: other people's children were pleasant but fundamentally uninteresting to me. The idea of breastfeeding made me squeamish. I never wanted to hold other people's babies, partly out of a fear of doing it wrong, but also because I felt no connection to them. People would present them to you, and watch for the wave of hormonal bliss that was supposed to wash over you. I would scrunch my face and make a high-pitched sound that seemed socially acceptable, then hand the baby back as quickly as possible. I felt nothing towards these infants. I was delighted for their parents, their joy filled me with warmth, but a maternal reaction to their children was entirely absent. And as I progressed through my twenties into my thirties, that absence began to worry me. My partner and I shared a broad understanding that we wanted children. I don't remember when we first discussed this, but we both knew it was something that was on our agenda for our lives together, even if for much of our broke, stressed twenties it seemed a distant prospect. During those years, I waited for the broodiness to hit. 'It'll come,' said my mother, who started wanting children when she was in her late teens. But it never did come.

Other women close to me did not seem to share my conflicted view; they either wanted babies or they didn't. And so it was difficult to articulate my worries, which, if misunderstood, would place me in one of two camps that are so often cast in opposition to one another: the selfish women who want children, and the selfish women who don't want children.

One of my worries was that if I was deficient in the hormones that caused broodiness, I might also lack the chemistry to bond with my child. Perhaps the baby would fail to respond to me, and we'd end up saddled with each other forever in mutual cold tolerance. That day in the hospital waiting room, after my escape from Rasputin, I texted a friend who had kids. 'What if the baby hates me?'

'Why would the baby hate you?' he responded. 'Babies don't hate their parents. That comes later.'

I thought often about the birth, the mysterious destination everything in my life had pivoted towards. I tried to identify exactly what I was looking forward to. When my partner and I talked about our life with the child, our conversations focused on recreating happy memories from our own childhoods. We would read the child the Narnia books, then *The Hobbit*, then when they got older we would advise them to just skip Tom Fucking Bombadil in *The Fellowship of the Ring*. Library trips, Halloween, Christmas – traditions reconstructed, improved upon. We are both the children of divorced parents. It didn't strike me at the time, but I understand now that we were thinking of the birth of this child as a journeying back, rather than a journeying forwards.

3

The puddle that dripped onto the hallway floor as I carried my plate back to the kitchen was another clue that something was amiss, but I didn't do anything about it. It was such a tiny amount of fluid, and the internet assured me that small amounts of fluid loss are relatively normal in the later weeks of pregnancy. I didn't want to be one of those panicky women, forever in and out of the hospital in their final weeks of pregnancy. It had been drilled into us in antenatal classes not to go to hospital until the contractions were five minutes apart. When I thought about labour itself, what frightened me was the thought that at some point I would panic to the extent that I would lose control. Staying home seemed the best way to avoid confronting this prospect. I decided to cut the grass in the back garden.

My partner was at a work event in Malahide Castle, a thirty-minute drive away. After I emptied the grass collector into the brown bin and checked my underwear again, I gave him a call.

'I think I might be in labour. But there might be something a bit wrong – no contractions, but I think my water could be breaking. I think that's not the right way round?'

'Jesus. OK, I'm getting in the car now.'

'Well I'm not sure, so if you're in a meeting or something, maybe wait –'

'Jess! I'm getting in the car now!'

We drove through the mellow afternoon, down Parnell Street towards the Rotunda. The street ahead was a clear, wide vista strewn with blown rubbish, the blackened curve of the old Ambassador theatre sheltering a couple of men drinking cans. As we were stopped in traffic outside Fibber's, a director I know spotted me and ambled across to the open car window. 'I've just heard you're pregnant! Congrats!'

'Yes!' I said. 'I actually think I might be in labour now. We're just headed to the Rotunda.'

38
the DUBLIN REVIEW

He looked stricken.

'Oh I'm grand!' I said. 'Probably a false alarm.'

In the Rotunda they didn't seem to think I was grand. I'd started to feel some light cramping on the way to the hospital. They whisked me into a side room, and hooked me up to a monitor. They stripped me from the waist down. My waters were definitely breaking now, and there was so much of it; it started to get all over the floor and I kept dabbing at it with a roll of tissue. The midwife who was with me said there was meconium in the water. This was not a good sign: it usually meant the baby was in some distress. But the baby's heart rate was normal.

I told her my partner's name and she went to get him. A few minutes later, a strange man burst into the room and looked me right between the legs. 'Is this not your husband?' asked the nurse. It turned out my partner had heard his name called, but had sat down again when this other man had stood up.

We were moved to a ward and given some food before the inevitable induction; even though my contractions had started, meconium in the water meant we needed to deliver the baby as soon as possible. I ate some lamb stew, a decision I would regret for the next twelve hours. 'King Kunta' by Kendrick Lamar was stuck in my head, the hook going round and round. To pass the time, and work through the early contractions, we invented a game called Undergraduate Interpretative Essay, whereby we translated the lyrics of Lamar's (almost unbearably funky) track into earnest academic jargon.

In the birthing room, the lights were low. My right hand was resisting cannulae, and the grotesque sight of it swelling up with blood under the skin was a welcome distraction from the discomfort of the accelerated contractions. I'd been brainwashed by my yoga class into thinking epidurals were for people who don't know how to breathe, so I sucked on the gas tube offered, which made me feel nauseated: another welcome distraction from the pain. Every couple of hours, a doctor came in to do an 'examination' – like what vets on TV do to cows. The pain of this was the most unbearable: the only pain throughout which brought with it the blinding white panic I feared most, and the powerful urge to roll off the bed and escape. The hours spent in the strange treacle-light of the birthing room have all run together in my mind, but at some point the midwife on duty had to go home. She was very apologetic and said she hoped she would see me and the baby when her next shift started. As dawn light began to gather behind the room's drawn blinds, an obstetrician came in again for an examination. I was dilated enough to begin pushing. But the midwife drew her attention to the monitor, to the contraction readings being scratched onto the paper. I wasn't paying much attention. Tiredness had come over me, a resignation that felt dangerous, like the warmth that hypothermia brings. *Is this death?* I wondered as a number of new concerned faces drifted in and out of the room. The contractions were lessening, despite the oxytocin being fed into a drip in my arm.

As morning broke I was wheeled out of the low-lit delivery room into a surgical suite. The lights swam and jolted above me, and a masked and gowned man arrived and made an official-sounding announcement as to what was happening, repeating himself until he was sure I understood and could consent: the baby's heart rate was dropping, so they'd have to intervene. They were going to administer an epidural, then try a ventouse delivery. This would involve attaching a kind of suction cup to the baby's head and pulling, while I pushed. If this didn't work, they would immediately begin an emergency C section. The football team of people on one side of the room were identified as the surgeons who would carry out the operation if the ventouse failed.

After the examinations and the hours of contractions, the epidural was a relief. Once it took effect, the doctor told me to push, and I did, although with my body numb from the waist down I might just have been yelling. There was no pain, but the feeling of a root deep within me being pulled, accompanied by a sense of panic and the urge to ask, politely but urgently, if the doctor was sure he wasn't accidentally removing my pelvis? Just as the words formed, my daughter emerged, and was placed on my chest. Her eyes were strangely black. Her face was beautiful, but not human. The sense that there was nothing I could do to comfort her, no gesture or word she could understand, hit me like a dumbbell to the chest. She looked at me with the resignation of an animal about to be put to sleep.

Then panic erupted. My daughter was taken away and her lungs vacuumed. I didn't look, but her screams were terrible. Then she was given antibiotic injections. I was told I wouldn't see her for a few hours. I had heard so much about the importance of skin-to-skin bonding, of not removing the vernix too soon. But there was no room for any of that to be expressed; we still seemed to be in the midst of an emergency. The room emptied very quickly, leaving just two masked and gowned women, tidying and wiping away the blood.

'I'm sorry,' I asked, 'but could you tell me if they had to cut me?'

'Of course they did,' one of the women said. They went back to chatting to each other then, and left.

4

In the blurred hours after the birth, alone in the hospital bed, a strange dissatisfaction took hold of me. The morphine gave the light a brittle, glass-like edge. I was exhausted, but wide awake. 'King Kunta' was still stuck in my head. The dissatisfaction I felt was not connected, in my mind, to the circumstances of the birth, or the fact that my baby had not yet been returned to me. It was around a continuation of consciousness: the fact of the rest of the day and the next stretching ahead of me.

When my daughter was brought back, asleep, I took photos of her face. I lifted her carefully when she finally woke, and tried to feed her. She lolled away from my breast, too exhausted to latch. A nurse grasped my breast and levered it towards my daughter's mouth, with no results. She brought me a tiny syringe and I tried to hand express some colostrum. No one mentioned the availability of a pump or a lactation consultant. After half an hour, I managed to express a tiny amount by hand. The nurse came back, congratulated me, then told me I needed to work until I had around ten times the amount. Instead I fell asleep, waking later when my partner was allowed back in to visit. He brought me a bunch of books that he'd bought in Chapters on his way in. For some reason I found the sight of them distressing: it was such a nice gesture, but when would I have the time to read them? A few hours later he had to go again, and I was left alone for the night.

When I woke later that night, my daughter was screaming. I tried to get her to latch again, but couldn't. Eventually a nurse came in to find me crying hysterically – the baby had not fed properly since birth that morning. She brought in some formula, and the baby fed and fell back asleep. The nurse looked at me strangely. Something in my reaction was clearly unsettling her, but I couldn't tell what. They took the baby away for a while, to the nurses' station, so I could sleep. An hour later I heard her screaming again and they brought her back. Finally she latched, but the pain was immediate and intense and soon my nipples were bleeding. After she finished feeding, I lay in the bed, stunned. The sound of babies crying echoed throughout the wards, each new cry unleashing a new surge of adrenaline into my exhausted system.

The immediate future stretched out ahead of me like a desert. I was connected to a catheter bag that was overflowing, and bleeding now from both groin and nipples. My legs were still sluggish from the epidural. I was terrified and clearly failing, already, at being a mother. There was, I perceived, a vast gulf of time to be survived before the tiny vulnerable baby in the cot beside me became the blurry child-shaped presence I'd imagined. I hadn't thought how I would fill those years of vulnerability, of need. I'd neglected to set aside enough of myself to give. And in this strange panicked state between sleeping and wakefulness, my mind suggested a solution that spun around my drowsy brain – the idea that the easiest thing now would be for my consciousness to inhabit my daughter: that I could swap my thirty-three-year-old body for a new body and start life all over again. Then someone could take care of us both, someone better equipped than I was. I lay half asleep in the tangle of hospital sheets, urine dripping slowly into a bag, and waited for my consciousness to shift into that of the sleeping baby by my side.

When I woke the next morning, this idea lingered in the back of my brain. I understood the oddness of it, its lack of rationality, and yet it persisted, like an off-key phrase of music stuck on repeat. A woman arrived with a form for me to fill out, a questionnaire about reactions to the birth experience. I dutifully completed it, and in response to the question 'Have you felt overwhelmed since the birth?' I ticked 'Y' for 'Yes'. What I didn't write in the 'other comments' section was: *There has been some mistake. With this birth, I was meant to start my life again from infancy, but now I appear to be the owner of a torn and battered body and a tiny baby.*

The woman read the form and looked at me with concern. 'We'll have to put you on the watch list for post-natal depression,' she said, 'because you say here you've felt overwhelmed.'

Then the doctor who had delivered my daughter came in. I didn't recognize him at first, without his mask and gown and halo of surgical lights. He picked up my chart and flicked through it. 'The problem with your delivery was shoulder dystocia,' he said. 'This means the shoulders were too big and the baby got stuck. Why was this baby so big? Is there a weight issue here?' He gestured at me when he said the word 'here'. 'Is there a diabetes issue?'

'I think you'll see from my chart that there isn't,' I said. 'I did ask if the baby was too big.'

'Well, if you have another, it can't get so big,' he said. 'The next time, you will have to be induced two weeks early.' He left.

The next day, after finishing the course of antibiotics I'd been put on as a precaution, I was allowed to go home. It was the day of the All-Ireland football final, and as we drove towards our house, the Ballybough Road was overrun. We inched the car forward through herds of men, women and children shouting and waving flags, pressing against the car's side windows.

At home, I waited for my milk to let down and tried to feed my daughter. Her latch impulse was poor, and my nipples were so excruciatingly sore that even my clothing brushing against them sent daggers of pain shooting through me.

My parents called round to help, but I didn't have the energy to communicate what help I might need. My mother assured me that the milk would arrive, everything would be fine. This seemed to be my breaking point. I screamed at her: 'But right now, there is no fucking milk. Do you understand? There is NO FUCKING MILK.'

She flinched in a way that struck me as being just like my daughter's startle reflex. And I took some pleasure in the brief illusion of control her alarm gave me.

The next morning, the public health nurse arrived to show us how to bathe the baby. After washing her gently, she swirled my daughter's dark, curly hair into a little puff on top of her head. We wrapped her in a beautiful stripy blanket and took photos of her with her poor squished head poking out to send to friends. Afterwards, I wanted the public health nurse to check my stitches, which was something I'd been told she was supposed to do.

'I'm sure they're fine,' she said.

'I'd like you to check.'

We went upstairs and I pulled down my leggings and lay down sideways on my bed. She looked from a distance and said the stitches were, indeed, fine. It was intensely humiliating. For the rest of the visit, hoping to prove I was normal and not a hypochondriac and not insane and not giving up on breastfeeding, I gabbled my plans for the future at her with a mania that probably bumped me from 'watch-list' to 'code red'. That night, I woke with a fever and swollen breasts – my milk had finally arrived, but my next attempt at feeding resulted again in profusely bleeding nipples. I resigned myself to a mixture of breastmilk (pumped via a cheap machine we'd bought online) and formula. The fact that I couldn't, or didn't want to, push through the pain of breastfeeding filled me with a heavy guilt.

5

The rest of our lives began. My daughter and I got by just fine. By which I mean that for those first months we existed, together, moving through time in an undeniably chronological fashion. Come 4.30 in the afternoon, I would sit on the sofa, staring out the window, waiting for my partner's car so I could hand my daughter to him and go lie down in my bedroom, alone. He would come in, able to give to her the joy and generosity the hours had stripped from me.

My mother called to the house often with offers of help I didn't know how to accept. The delusion of rebirth had spread to my thinking about her too. I'd become seized by the anxiety that somehow I had stolen time from her life to give to the baby; that this introduction of new life to our family tree had sapped strength from its roots. I pictured my mother thinning, losing her corporeality. Somewhere in my lizard brain lurked the concept that a bargain had been struck: in exchange for the baby and me surviving our labour, something had to be taken. Again my rational brain worked hard to dismiss this Faustian notion, but the anxiety continued to lurk, exhausting me.

In those early months I tried to tease out the strands of my cognitive dissonance. I found myself in an unexpected state of mourning which seemed to be sparked by the realization that in becoming a parent, my own child-hood was finally, irrevocably behind me. Perhaps that was where the odd desire to take my daughter's place as the infant in our lives had come from? I found myself flooded with memories of childhood tinged with a strange finality, a sense that it was time to close a door on them forever: the concrete schoolyard with its cotoneaster hedges warped out of shape by hundreds of children, the half-remembered piano lessons, disappointing school trips to the zoo and grey afternoons spent at home reading. Memories of the house I grew up in that was lost in the divorce. And my earliest memory: my legs poking out from beneath the buggy's waterproof bubble, a soft rain soaking through my socks and my irritation at my mother's stupidity in forgetting to tuck my feet in.

I was mourning a childhood I hadn't really enjoyed. I adored my parents, and had a particularly close connection with my mother: the sort of connec-tion I hoped to have with my daughter. But I was an only child and never understood the rules of interaction. I veered between wanting to be involved in everything and wanting to be left alone. These mixed impulses made me easy to exclude.

One of my earliest memories is of walking alongside the park across the road from my house. I must have been going to or from a friend's house. But my friends were not in their houses; they were hiding behind the hedge that ran along the park railings, and laughing at me. They were ghosting my foot-steps with their own, their giggles floating above the overgrown lilac and hawthorn. This was a game one local girl would periodically co-opt us all into, in order to exclude one member of the group. Because I would not play, I was the one alone on the other side of the hedge, chest hurting with the unfairness of it all. When I think back on childhood friendships, most mem-ories are of difficulty, and hurt, the sense of looking for something that the other children couldn't give me: the complete companionship of a sibling.

In those late autumn months, as my daughter and I settled into a routine,

I would wander the neighbourhood with her strapped against me in a harness, where she would bawl and struggle until the warmth of my body sent her to sleep. Or I'd push her for hours in her buggy through Fairview Park, or all the way into town on some pointless errand. Autumn fell around us in drifts of gold that slowly mouldered into the shitty dregs of November, but still I walked, around and around, with nothing to do except talk to a sleeping baby. A measles outbreak on the north side of the city made me afraid to take public transport with her and so we stayed on foot, through rain and cold, walking and walking and getting nowhere.

Sometimes I would sit on a bench and watch her sleeping in her buggy. She was fascinating, but unknowable. *This is fine*, I'd think. But she could be frightening at times. She didn't particularly like to be picked up or handled. People would visit, around the time she was starting to smile and goo, and I would warn them that she didn't want to be held. She liked being talked to, and bounced in her bouncy chair, and read to, but she didn't necessarily want to be in anybody's arms. They would look at me like I was insane, pick her up, and then look at me with even more concern when a bloodcurdling wail would erupt from her.

Friends and relatives visited in those first days and all remarked she was an easy baby – no colic, no reflux – but sometimes she would cry and nothing would stop her. All babies cry, of course. But my daughter had a cry so loud that people in cafés dropped their cups in alarm. I would pick her up, then put her down again, as though I was placing a pin back in a grenade. You can't reason with an infant. Perhaps I was a little jealous of this, her licence to be unreasonable. Or I was afraid that the anger in her was something I had given her. And maybe I wanted to go back, carrying with me all my reason, all the knowledge I have picked up on how to manage the things and people that would hurt her, and implant this knowledge in her life, while simultaneously fixing my own.

I checked the internet constantly for developmental milestones – to capture some sense of the passage of time, of achievement, some sense that these doldrum days would not last forever and that eventually I would not be tethered to a tiny baby. On my phone in the kitchen, my daughter sleeping on my shoulder, I'd scroll; moving from room to room in the small house, the chill of time spent indoors settling in my bones. With winter stealing light outside the window, a little more each day, I'd read updates on child development, fixes for flat-head syndrome, *tummy time, tummy time, tummy time*, as the baby screamed, face down, on the tummy-time mat. I haunted bizarre parenting forums, places of suppressed violence that often simmered over into threads festering with blame. Nothing in them allayed my anxiety, my sense that some important step in the process leading from birth to bonding to best existence had been missed.

Websites on post-natal depression were less insidious, but still frustrating. I'd read them sneakily in the evenings on my phone screen while pretending to watch TV. The symptoms they listed were so banal, so quotidian – sadness, anger, anxiety, tiredness – that on reading them I began to suspect I had been suffering with post-natal depression all my life. Perhaps, having been born with post-natal depression, and giving birth in turn, I had compounded my sadness, anger, anxiety, tiredness to unbearable levels. Why did I have this fantasy of starting anew? Why this sense of devastation at having to live in my own body? I thought back to that time during labour when the warmth of exhaustion had flooded me, taking all choice and agency out of my hands.

Often when I am distressed, I try to calm myself through the process of logically probing my emotional responses – the mental equivalent of breathing into a paper bag. The constant rational voice in my head, the dispassionate observer who's never left me even in my worst moments, can be a curse. This voice is judgemental, hard, inflexible. It's like a third parent with no patience, and it's this voice I fear most when I come close to losing control. But it's also the voice that speaks to me, low and quiet, during moments of panic, and never quite becomes lost in the white noise. I cleaved to it during these months of emotional and hormonal turbulence, and used its logic to explore the meaning of what I was experiencing.

Another breakthrough was my discovery of a further symptom on the post-natal depression websites. 'Intrusive thoughts' are not listed on every website, but they seemed to me a clever and simple way to define what I'd been experiencing; the tug of war between the primal, hormonal fears around death and rebirth and the flat monotone of the voice that told me my anxieties were all nonsense. 'Intrusive thoughts' is a good way of describing the kind of anxiety that forces you to imagine all of the terrible things that might happen to the people you love in minute detail. It's the voice that counsels violence in reaction to frustration. It may be posited as an 'intrusion' to make you feel better – to suggest that somehow this voice has nothing to do with you. But in truth it is the nasty aspect of you, the part of you of which you are ashamed. It is the voice in your head you remember that called your mother stupid as she pushed you in your buggy and sang adoring songs to you. Like a broken bone that's healed wrong, it's ugly, fused. But unlike a broken bone, it can't be reset.

I think I had imagined my life, post-partum, as being indistinguishable from my child's: that we would somehow inhabit the same consciousness, but remain separate. I would see the world through her eyes, interpret it for her, warn her of danger, and along the way right any of the wrongs that had befallen me. Perhaps this delusion is a particularly only-child way of completely misunderstanding the simple act of reproduction. But I realized this, at the very least, was what I had expected childbirth to offer me: this closeness. I had expected there to be an immediate bond of sweet, pure love that would tie us together, that would unite us in an understanding of the world.

Of course, this closeness is denied us, as it should be. The only inalienable right in this world, the only privacy we have not managed to obliterate for each other, is that of individual consciousness. The websites tell you that this sense of aloneness in consciousness is 'numbness', and that this numbness will melt away once the child is older, and more interesting, and the parent gets to know it. The terrible shallowness of this is difficult to accept.

And yet. It becomes hard to remain caught up in this circuit-course of misery when your baby is clapping her hands and hooting. When she has her father's inherent likeability to balance the flare-ups from the maternal line. When her hair is so mystifyingly copper-coloured, like no one else's in the family, and her face is so of her own making. When there is no journeying back, only forward.

Now, when my daughter and I are alone, she folds into me, because she needs to. And I will continue to age, my body will continue to be injured, and recover more slowly, and for some golden years my daughter's orbit and my own will intersect in a closeness that is special, because it is fleeting. I picture this process as spheres shifting slowly towards each other in the night sky far above us, and as I do so I feel my daughter's head droop onto my shoulder, see her grey eyes unfocus. She is with me, and also a thousand miles away: mind in flight over some far shore. The privacy that exists even in our most intimate moments allows me to sing my songs to her, flush with love, while she may well be forming pre-language criticisms in that unknowable mind of hers. I am relieved that I will never, can never, intrude upon those thoughts. And I am relieved that, along with whatever flaws I may unwillingly gift her, she will take from me what she needs, as I took what I needed from my mother, and she from hers.

Father and son

NATHAN DUNNE

The teacher loomed above the class to declare that the history of modern Ireland is the history of young men. And history, remember, especially the history of young men (he would stare at Sully, unwavering, as though to say *young men like you*), is never just history. It is each name and face and shape of each man's shoe as he treads, and where he treads, the footprint he leaves, and how he, the one man, becomes they, the many men. Boys, do you understand?

History is not a line that can be drawn from one battle to another. You must see that to push is eventually to force, and to force is inevitably to fight. And young men have fought many fights. How have they fought? Knife fights, gun fights, Tommie-fights, Thracian fights, dogfights. Do you know what a dogfight is? Look here, sit up boy, and stop dreaming or you'll be dumb as'n oxen on market day.

What's a market day, Father?

Questions, however inane or obtrusive, would make the teacher earnest.

Well, that's an interesting question.

What's an oxen, Father?

You know what oxen are, McCready. They are the plural – one plus another – of an ox.

What's an oxen, Father?

Sully's father left him for the last time on September 20, 1962. He'd been skulking in the bedroom all afternoon. Sully had gone in to ask if he'd like to eat his eggs in the front room or if he should bring them in. His father's body was turned away from the door, smoke rising from the ashtray where he had balanced a cigarette. There was the heavy smell of liquor. He said to forget about the eggs and to close the door and sit down. When Sully sat on the floor across from him with his knees arched, as he'd done since childhood, his father shook his head and said 'Hopeless' and had him stand up again. He said he wasn't like his brother. Sully stood silent. He asked him to open the dresser drawer and pick out the book that had a tea-stained yellow cover. Ernie O'Malley. *On Another Man's Wound.*

'Open it up to the first page, to the introduction. I know you're a reader, son. Read it out.'

Sully had only ever read aloud for school or church, and the experience was always nauseating. The idea of reading in front of his father, who himself worked with few syllables, seemed even worse. 'But I –'

'Go on. It's only me here.'

Sully, with a slight tremor in his fingers, began to read. 'This book is an attempt to show the background –'

'No, no. Skip down. To the second part.'

A passage in pencil had been underlined. 'My attitude towards the fight is that of a sheltered individual drawn from the secure seclusion of Irish life to responsibility of action. It is, argh, sorry, it is a narrative against the backgrounds of the lives of the people. The tempo of the struggle was –'

'Read slower now. Much slower.'

Sully coughed at the smoke before continuing. 'Life went on as usual in the middle of tragedy and we were intimately related to this life of our people. The people's effort can be seen only by knowing something of their lives and their relationship to our underground government and armed resistance. We who fought effected a small ... a small part of the total energy. This is not a history. Dates I considered unimportant. Our people seized imaginatively on certain events, exalted them through their own expression in song and ... argh, song and story. These are what concern me, my part and theirs, and my changing relation to them.' At the bottom of the page there were initials – *E. OM.* – and a date: 1931–34.

'See what he's saying there?'

'I'm not sure,' Sully said.

'They have a fire, those words.'

His father lit another cigarette, tapped his lighter on the side of the bed. 'Like your Uncle Ogden said when he told me to read this book, most memoirs of 'RA members aren't any good. It's all "Then we blew up the lorry and hid in the bushes." Or it's "I was a wee fat lad. I drank and drank and then I shot someone." But O'Malley can actually write.'

Sully nodded, breathing in his father's voice.

'Every road you walk down, every shop, every postbox, it's all controlled by the Brits. And voting changes nothing, they have it rigged, tied up in advance. They'll never leave Ireland unless we make them, unless we push them out.'

That night, Sully was asleep when his father raised the latch on the gate.

In the morning he awoke early to commotion downstairs. The uneasy clank of cutlery. Taps turned on and off with force, blasted then withheld. When he and Fergus appeared, having raced down the stairs in their socks, Uncle Ogden was embracing their mother in the front room. He was wearing blue overalls, having come straight from a job. His eyes were restless. He patted the boys hard and drew them in. Sully and Fergus didn't look at one another. They were told to sit down.

As Uncle Ogden came to the words 'Your Da is dead', their mother broke down and moved away from them, hiding her face. Sully called after her as she moved into the kitchen, but Uncle Ogden held out his palm.

Surveying the room in a panic, Sully's eyes fell on his father's church shoes resting on a sheet of newspaper, having been shined the day before. The brush lay by them, its bristles still lightly caked with polish.

On the day of the funeral, men came to the door. Sully only faintly recognized them. His mother spoke to the men quietly and it was explained to him and Fergus that they would help Uncle Ogden carry the coffin. Each of the men wore ironed black trousers with black jackets zipped to the top. Their starched collars concealed scars or tattoos or rose-hued birthmarks. They were solemn, with sallow cheeks and plain polished wedding rings (although one of them made a joke about a 'Cockdipper'). Sully looked at them carefully, and then again. Their tight-lipped expressions and short answers were familiar to him.

One of the men turned to the two boys. 'He was a good man, your Da,' and the others chimed in, 'A good man.'

From out of the church they began as a small procession, moving up the hill by the clock above News & Bait. Uncle Ogden walked as lead pallbearer, flanked by the men in black jackets. Their mouths were taut. Sully and Fergus walked either side of their mother, although she never looked down at them. Her eyes were lost. A light rain fell, its mist forming a thin film on Sully's face. Cars slowed at their edges. Inside the cemetery gate others joined them. The group swelled to about thirty and Sully saw his mother draw further within herself at the larger crowd. She pulled on her jacket and began to shiver. Uncle Ogden gave her an umbrella.

When they lowered the coffin, Sully was shocked at the narrowness of the grave: a whole life only worth this small cut in the earth.

Inevitably, church bells in the distance rang through the weak foliage.

The walls of the house were never so thin as after his father had gone. He would lie curled in bed trembling at the sound of his mother's crying from the room down the hall. Ten steps. That's all it had ever taken. His parents' bedroom had been a still compartment, a safe pocket. The lamp by the bed. The scratched chest of drawers he was never to touch. A coffee stain on the beige rug that had been brushed and cleaned but never erased. His father's rough shape beneath the bedsheets on a Saturday afternoon, heavy rain wetting the roof outside.

On the third night, his mother wailed suddenly and brokenly. He and Fergus ran to her bed and sat by her. They brought tea and water and salt biscuits. But she refused them and they sat growing cold and stale at her side. Her hair was cold. The skin on her forehead stretched tight and glossy, a twisted blue vein pressing on the surface.

By the end of the week she wouldn't leave her bed. The doctor came and gave her a bottle of pills. Grey circles grew darker beneath her eyes. Fergus went out to drink and Sully was left alone with her. He sat on a chair by the chest of drawers and watched her sleep. She slept so silently he would occasionally get up and bend down to see if she was still breathing. It was as though her body, still beating, was an affront to his death, where the only acceptable response was paralysis.

Sully dreamt of a thin magic light that he could place down inside her that would light up her eyes and skin and make her head warm and tender and when she opened her mouth she would say, 'Sully, let's dance.' And they would dance around the room and knock into furniture and open the curtains and let the light flood in and sing a song from his childhood.

They soon learned his father's death had been an accident. No barracks raid or bomb plot. No guns. Only a car, alcohol and speed. His father had left Appleroddy's Bar shortly after eleven with Lewis Breen and Sean McVerry, also volunteers. They must have driven fast from the area because the police report, which Sully glimpsed years later among his mother's bank statements, recorded a Mrs Maguire of Brookvale Street who had heard a terrifying noise.

MRS MAGUIRE: The car exhaust was banging and I looked out to see it smoking, from the exhaust.

SGT HATTON: Would you say the car was backfiring then?

MRS MAGUIRE: Aye. There was singing too, from the car. I could hear their voices.

On many nights he would imagine his father moments before the crash. He saw him in the driver's seat, singing, his lips still wet with bourbon. His face was animated: brow wrinkled, a wide smile, the gap between his front teeth clearly visible. His back was arched and, after a hump in the road, his body slightly raised from the seat. There was no seatbelt. As the others joined him in song he took the corner too fast, and when they emerged onto the outer road from the bend the speed gathered around them and made Lewis in the back begin to laugh at the thrill of pressing harder along the flat. His father felt the thrill and nodded a little on the pedal to head away from the buildings, whose shadows lifted higher at their tail, and as he tried to dodge the branch lying on the road the others reached a higher drunken note in the song to distract him. The right tyre hit the branch and sent the car reeling and skimming. Sully saw it in one total flash, the speckled square of light. The car hit a tree and his father's chest was crushed by the weight of the steering wheel.

For a moment, his father was still breathing. The engine whirled wild and hot and burned slowly down to silence. The twisted hunk of metal wrapped to the stubborn thick of a tree and his father dead inside, his body lost to the ruin. A wheel was missing.

When his father was pulled from the wreckage there was the blood of other men on his face.

In my parents' garage: a diary for 2020

IAN SANSOM

Monday 1 January

Watched *Los Dos Papas* last night on son's Spanish girlfriend's mum's Netflix account. (He was on the phone to her for hours – the girlfriend, not the mum. Rushed in at midnight asking for some grapes – something about the Spanish tradition of eating twelve grapes of luck? We had no grapes – of luck, or otherwise. Said hello to Spanish girlfriend and her mother on FaceTime. They were dancing and waving sparklers, popping grapes.) Portrait of the friendship between the Popes very moving.

Rather wish I was a Spanish Catholic – for New Year's, at least.

Old friends came round this afternoon, hadn't seen them for months. We shared midlife war stories: this year her father died, his mother died, their dog died, both their surviving elderly parents have serious dementia, and they're having trouble with their teenagers. Toasted the New Year.

Tuesday 7 January

The *Times*: 'Popcorn calamity': 'A firefighter needed open-heart surgery to fight a deadly blood infection after getting popcorn stuck in his teeth. Adam Martin, a 41-year-old father of three from Coverack in Cornwall, contracted endocarditis after damaging his gum when he used objects, including a piece of wire and a metal nail, in an attempt to dislodge the piece of food.'

Oven-cleaning man came. The oven has twenty years of baked-on dirt, despite my efforts with hot water, scourer and Mr Muscle. My wife has decided enough is enough. We need a professional.

The oven man says he was terribly sick over Christmas. Had never been so sick. Ended up in hospital with respiratory problems. He used to be a sales director for a big local firm, travelled the world, but now he's made enough money to quit and follow his dream – has bought his own woodland over on the Ards Peninsula and has big plans to replant native species. He does the oven cleaning for fun and to meet interesting people – 'like yourself, sir'.

Tuesday 14 January

Workload rather overwhelming: sheer volume. Like an endless puzzle. Have somehow ended up as Head of Department. Endless form-filling, reports, spreadsheets, meetings. If I'd wanted to end up in middle management I should really have gone into business. At the end of his working life in the quarries, my dad was managing the quarries. I realize I have effectively become a depot manager.

Sunday 2 February

The children have returned to college. Our first weekend alone in the house for a long time. Haven't quite adjusted: I still cook enough food for five people. My wife's new job is based in London so it's only me here during the week.

Big house for one person.

I work all day, return home at night, cook a meal for five for myself – or nothing at all, eating yesterday's leftovers – then tidy and clean, and go to bed early. I really need to start socializing and getting out more.

Friday 28 February

According to the local news, the first case of the new virus has been confirmed in Northern Ireland. They're shutting some towns in northern Italy. Eldest son was in northern Italy over the New Year with his girlfriend. When he came back he was terribly sick – off work – for two weeks. Flu.

Monday 2 March

Have never been to Killarney. Made a list of all the places I have never been in Ireland: the Cliffs of Moher, the Rock of Cashel, Blarney Castle, Kinsale, the Dingle Peninsula, Lough Derg, the English Market in Cork, the Aran Islands. Massive list. The sorts of places I imagine I might visit in retirement, on an Ulsterbus tour.

Was in England at the weekend with my wife, visiting my parents. There's no easy way to get to Killarney from Norfolk. Flew to Kerry with Ryanair from Luton Airport – took half a day's travel just to get to Luton. No one in their right mind wants to go anywhere with Ryanair from Luton. Airport packed.

By the time I reached Kerry Airport I was tired and hungry and the place was shutting up for the night and there was only a vending machine and I had no coins and the place was deserted. Had expected an actual airport, but it's more like a runway with a large shed attached. Taxis had to be pre-booked. Eventually got a bus.

Streets deserted as I made my way along the N71 to the hotel, mobile down to 2% battery, soaked to the skin. Hotel packed with people from all nations, perched at tiny tables in the lobby, eating vast plates of chicken goujons and drinking Guinness like there was no tomorrow.

Tuesday 3 March

There is a tomorrow. And tomorrow is today and today is the second day of the Citizen Ceremonies at Killarney Convention Centre. It's going to be the last one this year – because of the virus.

I first applied for Irish citizenship when I was working in Dublin a few years ago. It seemed only polite. But the process was so complicated and so expensive I let it lapse before I cleared the first couple of hurdles – lawyers, sworn witness statements. I gave up. But after Brexit, and with the children and my wife all proud Irish citizens, and half a lifetime here now, I redoubled my efforts.

Present myself at precisely 9.30 a.m. at the Killarney Convention Centre, with several thousand others. We snake through the building towards registration, where we are handed our naturalization certificates and then take our seats for the ceremony. I am seated next to a woman from Nigeria and a man from Italy. The Nigerian woman works in a nail bar in Dublin. The Italian is married to an Irishwoman. The Irish Defence Forces band strikes up with a medley of Beatles hits, there's the obligatory harpist, a few words from a TD, and then the flag is raised and we all pledge allegiance to the Irish state.

If you'd told me anytime over the past twenty-five years that I'd ever become an Irish citizen I wouldn't have believed you. No need. Not an Irish bone in my body. Nonetheless: quietly proud. Sense of acceptance.

Thursday 19 March
'It's now or never,' says my wife. Flybe has collapsed, British Airways are cancelling flights, panic buying has begun, and rumours of a London lockdown are circulating on social media. If I'm going to make it to England from Belfast to see my parents, I'm going to have to move pretty fast.

They are in their mid-eighties, my mum and dad – both smokers until recently, wary of fruit and veg, working-class Londoners who long ago ended up in the wilds of East Anglia.

'The Professor's here,' says my dad, on my arrival. They like to call me the Professor, or the Rabbi: they think it's funny.

'I won't come in,' I say.

'What do you mean you won't come in?' says my mum.

'The coronavirus,' I say.

'Lot of nonsense,' says my dad.

'You're meant to be staying inside,' I say.

'Boris'll sort it,' says my dad, who switched from Labour around about the time of Mrs Thatcher and has never looked back.

'Will you not come in for a cup of tea?'

'I'd better not,' I say, and head straight for the garage, where I intend to set up camp for the foreseeable.

My wife has returned home from London to NI; the children are returning from college.

Monday 23 March

I have just about everything I need here. About eighteen months ago we decided to convert the garage into somewhere for me to stay when I'm over: a wood-burning stove, a tiny little bed, a desk, a hob, a sink. It's better than staying in the spare room: none of us would last a week if I was in the spare room.

'This is your dream, really, isn't it,' says my wife. 'Like your own little Hobbit house.' It's OK – view of the river, view of the shed, view of the other shed. But Bag End it is not: it's my mum and dad's garage, with a window.

In addition to the stove and the bed and the desk I have an emergency stash of books: charity-shop crime mostly, plus some old A-Level textbooks that have somehow made it through every one of my mother's relentless culls, and a selection of miscellaneous non-fiction collected over the years and abandoned here, including Graham Greene's dream diaries, and the second volume of Isherwood's *Diaries*.

Last year I spent about four months working with my friend W on an adaptation of Defoe's *Journal of the Plague Year*. My agent said it needed work and didn't send it out. 'Worth trying again?' asks W.

Irish friend texts – he's heard I went through the naturalization process. 'Alright, Irish?'

Thursday 26 March

Last night a friend brought me a massive palm tree.

'I know what that is,' I say.

'I know you know what that is,' he says, but neither of us actually says what it is, and he then leaves, going round the back of the house, by a route I am not familiar with, and I follow him, out onto the streets of what seems to be a small Scottish fishing village and all the way back to my front door.

And then I woke up.

Everyone's dreaming more, apparently. There have been articles in the papers and online; they've been talking about it on *Woman's Hour* on Radio 4; lockdown dreams being recorded, collected and curated for future reference; an important account of our imaginative and emotional lives during these – what everyone now refers to as – 'unprecedented times'.

Saturday 28 March

A week in, and I am adjusting to what everyone is now referring to as 'the new normal'. My new normal is working all day, hunched over my laptop in the garage or the shed – which acts as a sort of annexe to the garage, a makeshift study cleared of tools, view over the river in the distance – or wandering down the road to get a signal on my phone for meetings, then cooking for my parents, who mostly doze and potter around all day.

This evening I made my celebrated mince on toast – my parents' favourite meal among my dozen or so staples. I leave the meals on the back doorstep for them. My mum – who has an autoimmune disorder – picks up the plates wearing Marigolds and maintaining a safe distance, and I then shuffle off to eat alone in the garage, reading in bed till late.

The second volume of Isherwood's diaries covers the 1960s, at which point he is living in Santa Monica, is famous and rich – though not yet rich enough to give up teaching – and remains devoted to his Vedanta guru Swami Prabhavananda. He is also weathering the continual storms of his relationship with the artist Don Bachardy, who was thirty years his junior, and with whom he was engaged – in his own words – in continuous 'psychological wrestling matches'.

Am engaged in psychological wrestling matches of my own. Suggested to my parents that we needed to get a plan together. My parents are not people who like being told what to do. They lived through the war, and left school early; my dad was in the Royal Marines and then the Special Boat Service. They are tough people with no more time for coronavirus than they have for do-gooders, know-it-alls, and anyone who tries to interfere. My dad scoffs at the suggestion he should stay two metres away from people.

'I don't even know what two metres is,' he says. 'What's wrong with good old English feet? That's why we voted Leave.'

Sunday 29 March

'Would you like a cup of coffee?' I ask my dad.

In response, he sings a song. I'd forgotten how much he loves to sing. Hymns, folk songs, John Denver, music hall. He starts singing 'All I Want Is a Proper Cup of Coffee'. I have heard him sing it a thousand times:

> *All I want is a proper cup of coffee*
> *Made in a proper copper coffee pot.*
> *You can believe it or not.*
> *I want a cup of coffee*
> *In a proper coffee pot.*
> *Tin coffee pots or*
> *Iron coffee pots*
> *They're no use to me.*
> *If I can't have a*
> *Proper cup of coffee*
> *In a proper copper coffee pot*
> *I'll have a cup of tea.*

So I make him a cup of tea.

Mid-morning, or mid-afternoon, I try to find time to sit outside with them in the garden. They drink tea. I drink coffee. They regard coffee as an affectation, something that you drink if you've been to university, though this has never stopped them from drinking it. When I was young they had a percolator and once a week – on a Sunday – they would produce the percolator in a ceremonial fashion and make this very weak, milky coffee, the way they still like it now.

'All that coffee'll kill you,' says my mum.

'Balzac died of drinking coffee,' I say.

'Who's Ack?' says my mum.

They reminisce about toilet tissue of old, Izal in particular. I recall going to my grandparents, where my granddad would patiently tear up old newspapers for toilet tissue.

In terms of stockpiling, my mum is not interested in toilet rolls, pasta or hand sanitizer. What she wants me to get, every time, are tins of evap, condensed milk and Golden Syrup. In case one of us is in danger of going into a diabetic coma.

Friday 3 April

There was a writer on the radio this week claiming that he had been self-isolating for years, and so was well prepared for the 'current crisis'. I don't know why I found this stupid and offensive, but I did. It wasn't funny. Also, I always want to believe that writers live the kind of life depicted in Paolo Sorrentino's *The Great Beauty*. Watched it again on my phone in bed last night, my own sad little cinema: Toni Servillo plays a writer, Jep Gambardella, whose life is a continual whirl of parties, dinners and soirées, a Christopher Isherwood kind of life. When things return to normal I am going to live more like Christopher Isherwood and Jep Gambardella.

Wednesday 8 April

Finding it more and more difficult to complete any work. It should be easier than ever: no commute, no distractions. But all the Microsoft Teams meetings and the Zoom and everything else has produced a kind of brain fog and a terrible lethargy. Also, the work itself seems pointless. I stare at my colleagues and students back in Belfast and they seem a million miles away.

Thursday 9 April

Everything has turned sinister. My mum wipes down the post wearing plastic gloves, using disposable wipes that have doubled in price; the police have been taping up park benches; streets are deserted; the American President is like something out of a Stephen King novel, or a J.G. Ballard; every absurd thriller plot and disaster movie set-up is suddenly plausible and real.

'I've been dreaming a lot recently,' I say to my mum.

'Are you secretly eating cheese?' she asks.

(My mum has always been highly suspicious of cheese – believing it to be the cause of all ills, both physical and psychological. I have been eating more cheese than usual. Cheese sandwiches pretty much every day. And 'Shall we have some cheese?' asks my dad, after every meal. To him – an evacuee, child of the London slums – the mere availability of cheese represents plenty and luxury. So why not eat the cheese now, when the chips are down, and damn the consequences.)

There's something called the 'clap for carers' at 8 p.m. on Thursday evenings. My mum and dad happily stand at the window and clap and shout. I don't know why it makes me embarrassed, but it does. I can hear the hollering and the banging of pots from next door. Honestly? I find it disturbing.

Friday 10 April

Back home in NI our next-door neighbour's daughter and her husband have had an offer on their house – and so they've come back to us with an offer to buy our house. Much less than market value. But we have been trying to sell the house on and off for about five years. My parents in England need looking after. My wife's job is – or was, and once again will be? – based in London. And we've got the garage.

We accept the offer.

Monday 13 April

Bank Holiday weekend – same as any other weekend. Made a half-hearted attempt at an Easter dinner for my mum and dad (couscous with lamb, a controversial choice – 'I prefer your mince on toast,' says my dad) – and later joined my wife and children back in Ireland via the House Party app, attempting to play some trivia game that had us all bored in minutes.

Christopher Isherwood's idea of a good night in, 8 January 1966: 'Allen Ginsberg came to supper with us, bringing his friend Peter Orlovsky and a seventeen-year-old boy named Stephen Boorstein. [...] Everybody got high, and Ginsberg recorded our conversation and chanted Hindu chants [...] All three of them are to some extent demon guests, harpies who descend and wreck the homes of the fat bourgeoisie with self-righteous malice.'

Wednesday 15 April

Government briefings. There is no TV here in the garage, no internet either, but I look up the briefings on my phone. The politicians look rather as if they're about to cry, or throw a tantrum.

Reading Isherwood, I don't feel quite so bad about my response to the pandemic. During the Cuban missile crisis – October 1962 – he writes, 'I feel such a curiously strong loathing of Castro – something to do with his beard, his sincere, liquid-eyed beard. I should like to see him forcibly shaved in the U.N.' Of the moon landing, 20 July 1969: 'The moon landing took place a couple of hours ago. Oh the horrible falseness of the commentator we heard.'

I seem to have taken offence at the government slogan 'Stay Home'. It sounds American. Surely it should read 'Stay at Home'?

Late at night now, when my parents have safely gone to bed, I've been watching TV on my phone, which I would never normally do. I have become obsessed with the Israeli series *Fauda* on Netflix, in particular those episodes in which Israeli counter-terrorist operatives sit around after some mission or other and smoke and drink and enjoy a barbecue together. We tried a barbecue here the other night but it was not the same as in *Fauda*: me and my mum and dad are not an elite IDF unit hanging out together after some daring operation. It was just us and some charred chicken in the back garden.

Saturday 18 April

Greene writes in the dream diaries: 'It can be a comfort sometimes to know that there is a world which is purely one's own – the experience of that world, of travel, danger, happiness, is shared with no one else.'

Maybe *this* is why we're all dreaming more: we may be self-isolating but we're also sharing the experience with the rest of the world and dreams are the only place untouched now by the virus, by governments, and by others. Our own private realms.

Eldest son was sacked from his job but then immediately reemployed with the announcement of the government furlough scheme. He's just moved into a flat with his girlfriend. I don't know what he'll do if he loses his job.

Monday 20 April

My mum says, on the doorstep, 'For the record, I do want to be resuscitated.' She has read something about calls being made to the elderly by GPs, asking something like: 'If you were to be admitted to hospital suffering from Covid, do you wish to be resuscitated?'. I say I'll make sure she is resuscitated.

'I don't think that means you just come back to life,' I say.

'I know that,' she snaps. 'I'm not stupid.'

Wednesday 22 April

Graham Greene's dreams feature Khrushchev, Castro, François Mitterrand and several Popes. My own fantastically vivid dreams feature mostly family and friends and occasionally the forgotten stars of TV shows of the 1970s and '80s: Richard O'Sullivan, Pat Coombs, Wendy Craig, and the other night the bloke who played Max (the butler? the chauffeur?) in *Hart to Hart*, starring Stefanie Powers and Robert Wagner. 'When they met, it was murder.' Is it because I'm living with my parents for the first time since the 1970s and '80s?

Friday 24 April

On the radio everyone's saying, 'Oh, the birdsong. I have heard the birdsong. It's a reminder of what we can learn from nature at this time of crisis,' etc.

'Those bloody pigeons,' says my mum, first thing every morning. And she holds up her hand as if cocking a pistol and makes a sound like 'Pugh, pugh, pugh,' as if shooting.

I remember, years ago, my eldest son when he was young asking my dad about his time in the Royal Marines, if he'd ever killed anyone, and my dad just laughed.

Graham Greene has dreams in which he is asked to assassinate Goebbels.

In last night's bird dream a giant pigeon came flying out of the bush by the kitchen and I was not quick enough with my gun: it soared off into the distance.

I am not convinced that we're not just destroying ourselves: some sort of collective death-wish.

Saturday 25 April

People are drinking more, according to the news. My parents are not big drinkers. My mum would occasionally have had a sherry or a glass of white wine – until the autoimmune disease. And my dad always used to drink this sweet, syrupy Manischewitz-style wine that he kept in the garage, but he now sticks to the occasional glass of supermarket Merlot, kept by the washing machine.

When I first met my wife's family in Ireland I was astonished at how much they would drink – Guinness, ales, whiskeys, wines. Vast quantities. Astonishing amounts. It was just what they did. I'd had absolutely no idea people lived that way. Alcohol had never been a part of my life.

It is now a part of my life, though even now I am at most a two-bottles-of-whiskey-a-year sort of a person: one bottle for Christmas and one for my birthday. Plus a couple of glasses of wine at the weekend. That would usually do me.

I've just got through a bottle of whiskey in a week.

Fortunately, from when he used to work in the quarries, my dad has a fine collection of spirits and liqueurs that people gave him, and which he's never touched: thirty or more years of nudge-and-a-wink Christmas gifts, from people who needed a tonne or two of aggregates, no questions asked. I have never been as glad to see a bottle of Tia Maria.

Monday 27 April

Every week my mum asks me to get them two loaves of bread – some 'floppy bread' and some 'proper bread'. The 'floppy bread' is a medium-sliced factory loaf, which my dad prefers.

For myself I buy a pack of those part-baked petit-pains – available in the corner shop – and I have one every morning, warmed in the oven. Tasteless, but suggestive of something. I don't know what – France, vaguely?

I leave them to do their own breakfasts. They get up much later than me. Sometimes my mum isn't up until 9 or 10, and my dad creeps around the house, trying not to make any noise, whispering to me and pointing upstairs – 'She's not right, you know.' But by the time she's had a shower and some breakfast she's usually all right. If he thinks he can get away with it, my dad will make himself a crafty sausage sandwich while my mum's still asleep.

If they're dining together for breakfast, they like a proper spread: cereals, jams, toast, and often scrambled eggs, which my dad does in the microwave. Their breakfasts last for an hour or more. I have no idea what they're up to in there. They're always laughing about something and the telly's always on – they have a telly in the kitchen and like to watch *Good Morning Britain*, with the subtitles on for my dad. They see nothing wrong with Piers Morgan: they take it all with a pinch of salt.

I, meanwhile, gobble my toast or my petit-pain with a cup of coffee around 6 or 6.30 a.m., standing up, staring aimlessly out of the window, listening to Radio 4, checking work emails. When it comes to breakfast, they have the right idea.

Saturday 2 May

Buy a newspaper. Haven't read a paper for weeks.

According to the government, we are now 'passing through the peak'. I don't believe it. They're promising to make one-off payments to families of frontline NHS and social care staff who died of Covid-19. A lot of bus drivers have died. What about the bus drivers?

Trump: 'And then I see the disinfectant, where it knocks it out in one minute. And is there a way we can do something like that, by injection inside or almost a cleaning?' Like everyone else, I have watched the clip on YouTube in disbelief half a dozen times.

Monday 4 May

Another vivid supermarket dream, in which I am making love to a beautiful woman in the bread aisle in our local Morrison's. Everyone just walks round us. Sometimes the woman is French, sometimes she is Italian. Sometimes I am French, sometimes I am Italian.

Thursday 7 May

Work is overwhelming. Online all day, then cooking for my parents, a bit of cleaning when they're safely in the front room. Completely exhausted at night. A friend has started sending me hilarious things on WhatsApp, which is not unwelcome. But where does he find the time?

House sale looks like it might go through. Selling a house during a lockdown not entirely straightforward. And house prices in England are rocketing – why?

Saturday 9 May

Years ago, at an apple fair, I asked a man at a stall selling apple juice if he had any cider. He said no, he wasn't allowed to sell cider at the apple fair, but just out of interest, how much would I want, if he did have some cider? I said I didn't really know – a bottle, just. He then reached down under the trestle table and produced a three-litre box of cider. 'That'll be £10 please.'

I've always dreamt of making my own cider – a townie's dream of rural life. Keeping chickens, making cider.

'What about planting some apple trees?' I suggest to my mum. There's a corner in the garden that would take a couple of trees.

'What on earth for?'

'For the apples.'

'What do we want apples for?'

'To eat?'

'You can buy apples in the shop,' she says, which is unarguable. There's been no apple shortage so far. My mum and dad only like Pink Lady apples – so sweet they taste like apple syrup.

'We could make our own cider,' I say.

My mum pulls a face, signalling disgust. She loves to pull faces.

'We'll call it Eileen's orchard,' I say.

'You can call it what you like,' says my mum. 'I won't be here to enjoy it.'

Sunday 10 May

I keep hearing the same stories again and again: my parents don't remember that they've told them before. The one about the bagel man – my dad pronounces it 'beigels', more 'aye' than 'eh'. Reminiscences about all the Jewish bakeries in the East End when he was growing up, how he and his brother used to buy pickled herrings on their way to school, from the herring man with his barrel. It always sounds like he's making it up – like it's something out of the 1930s. And then I realize, it *was* the 1930s.

Years ago, trying to Jew up a bit, I attempted to start cooking Jewish: honey-cake on Rosh Hashanah, matzah balls on Pesach, blintzes, latkes. But I was trying too hard. It wasn't my food – it wasn't our food.

'Shall I see if I can get some bagels?' I ask.

'No,' says my mum. 'Ugh. They're far too chewy.'

Saturday 23 May

My mum cleans her fridge at least once a week, even now – usually at the weekend. At home I'd usually clean the fridge about once every six months. My mum doesn't like an empty fridge. But she doesn't like a full fridge. It has to be just so. Fridge essentials for my mum are: Stork margarine, Dairylea cheese triangles, salad cream, and bacon for my dad.

Thursday 28 May

USA – just … I don't know what to say. A black man, George Floyd, died when a policeman knelt on his neck. It was filmed. Him saying, 'I can't breathe.' Protests and rioting in Los Angeles, Las Vegas, Denver, Portland, Dallas, Houston, Atlanta, Seattle, Phoenix, Pittsburgh, Philadelphia, New York, Boston – everywhere. Trump tweeted, 'When the looting starts, the shooting starts.'

Tuesday 30 May

'Non-essential' shops will be allowed to open from the 15th of June. Boris Johnson did not sack Dominic Cummings for having driven his wife and son from London to County Durham, even though you're not supposed to be doing that.

A plague of locusts in India.

Saturday 6 June

The government have extended the furlough scheme. Eldest son – and us – delighted.

House sale now going smoothly. Solicitors, etc.

Saturday 13 June

Black Lives Matter. In Bristol, a statue of someone called Edward Colston (1636–1721) – a merchant who grew rich from the slave trade – was thrown into the harbour. Part of me thinks, we don't do that sort of thing here. Part of me thinks, bravo. Sadiq Khan has announced a Commission for Diversity in the Public Realm to review London street names and statues.

I buy six bananas – four for me, two for my mum and dad. They don't eat a lot of fruit. Sometimes, in the old days, when I'd be visiting only every month or so from Ireland, my mum would have the same few apples in the fruit bowl, all year round, slowly rotting until I quietly threw them away and replaced them with fresh ones.

My dad's idea of eating more fruit is having bananas and custard.

'Shall we have bananas and custard?' he suggests, when he sees the bananas in the fruit bowl – a Pavlovian response. I haven't had bananas and custard for thirty years. I make bananas and custard. It is delicious.

Saturday 20 June

The statue of Winston Churchill in Parliament Square has been put into a wooden crate – for its own protection.

'Do you need anything?' I ask my parents every morning, standing on the doorstep, and every few days they'll both say, in unison, 'Eggs.'

They get through half a dozen eggs every couple of days. It's incredible.

'How come you're eating so many eggs?' I ask.

'They're cheap,' says my mum.

And they certainly are around here: within about a half-hour walk there are perhaps half a dozen houses with signs outside saying 'Fresh Eggs'. They're always a pound for half a dozen. Rural price-fixing.

'It used to be a pound a dozen,' says my mum.

The place I usually go to get the eggs my mum and dad call 'The Egg Man' – a farmer who's put an old shipping container by the side of the road, filled with crates and crates of eggs, and a little honesty box.

'People could nick them, but they don't,' says my dad, proudly. He likes to think of Norfolk as a kind of paradise – which in many ways it is. A paradise where people don't steal eggs from old shipping containers at the side of the road. Because the shipping container is equipped with CCTV.

Half a dozen brown eggs cost £1. Half a dozen white eggs cost 90p. I have no idea why.

'We only get the white. She' – says my mum, rather disapprovingly, about someone they used to buy eggs for, and who I now buy the eggs for – 'insists on the brown.'

Friday 27 June
Travelled back home, leaving my mum and dad with enough food for a month. Weird journey – no one around – and strange being back in NI. Haven't seen my wife in months. Celebratory meal – bread, cheese, bottle of sparkling wine.

We have a date for exchange and completion. All we need to do now is pack up the house. A lifetime's stuff.

Friday 24 July

Daughter works in an Irish bar in Scotland – which has finally reopened. Every day she gets abuse from people when she has to explain social distancing rules, masks, etc. – so bad that yesterday they had to call the police. Middle-aged men the worst, apparently – 'Don't tell me what I can and can't do, you f***ing wee bitch', etc. – and young women her own age.

Saturday 25 July

So, we sold the house. It was a good house. Great neighbours – none better. Park opposite and shops around the corner. Good dentist, good doctor, short walk to the school. Everything we needed.

When we arrived it was post-Good Friday Agreement and we were a young family: toddlers in tow, one on the way. And now we're gone, just the two of us – on the ferry yesterday. No big farewells. No party. No nothing. Because of the circumstances. Grim departure.

For me, living in that house represented the fulfilment of a dream. I gave up my job, started looking after the children in order to finally give writing a proper go. My wife worked full-time and I started writing in the evenings, when everyone had gone to sleep. It was all a bit of a gamble.

My wife spent most of lockdown packing and dividing up the spoils between the children. Who wants the spare grater? Who needs the old towels? All that remains is in storage now – everything we didn't sell or give away – and goodness knows when we'll see it again. I have my rucksack with just about everything I need: spare clothes, toothbrush, pencil, notebook, steel mug, charger, phone. My wife has two suitcases.

When the removal men had taken everything and the house was entirely empty I cried – and I mean really really wept. The realization that the house was just a house, ready for the next occupiers. We had served its purpose. We had no further role.

Friday 21 August

My last entry – and then the diary just stops for almost a month – is just a list of things to do before moving day. Gas and electricity. Clean bins. Paint. Instruction manuals. Clean.

My dad likes tongue-twisters almost as much as he likes to sing. I cook some fish. He says, 'A pleasant place to place plaice is a place where the plaice are pleased to be placed.' The fish is cod. And then he says: 'Fried fresh fish, fish fried fish, fresh fried fish, fresh fish fried, fish fresh fried.'

Honestly, what he could have achieved with an education, my dad. He'd have made an excellent Ian McKellen, or a Stephen Fry.

Once a week, in the good old days, every Friday my mum and dad would drive half an hour to a place called the Rembrandt, a fish and chip shop with a sit-in area and a little bar, off the A47. They loved the Rembrandt. It was a ritual. My dad would always have the haddock, with chips and mushy peas. My mum would usually have grilled sole, or whitebait.

'Do you think we'll ever make it back to the Rembrandt?' asks my mum, in doleful mood.

'Of course you'll make it back to the Rembrandt,' I say.

Monday 24 August

My wife and I are both living in the garage now. One room. The house back in Ireland was huge. We had it all set up. We had our friends. We had our jobs.

'What have we done?' I say to my wife.

'Don't start that,' she says. 'We've done what we had to do.'

My parents' sixtieth wedding anniversary. We were planning a big celebration – my parents have always loved a party. There were going to be people arriving from everywhere, friends, family, neighbours, former neighbours, entertainment by my sister, the gazebo in the garden, catering by yours truly. In the end it was just me, my wife and my mum and dad out on the patio with a cup of tea and a slice of cake. The only bit of hoopla was a video from my sister in Australia, which made my mum cry, and my wife got stung by a wasp. We did put up a bit of bunting – and my dad had a couple of glasses of the thick, sweet wine that he likes. Some phone calls from the grandchildren.

At the end of the evening, my mum got out the wedding album: padded, white, still in its presentation box, and kept as always in the sacred Schreiber side cupboard. I can remember looking at the album as a child and finding it difficult to recognize my parents in the images of rather exotic, glamorous young people: my mother impossibly slim and looking like Hedy Lamarr; my father slick and plush in his mobster suit, complete with pinkie ring and a full head of hair. I can see them perfectly clearly in those photos now. I'd missed it before: the characteristic twinkle in my dad's eye; my mum's look of determination; the laughter.

My mum starts going through the roll call of all the people in the big group photo. 'Ernest Ridley, dead. Florence Ridley, dead. Avril Ridley, dead.' George and Rhoda. George and Ivy. Will and Lil. Dead, dead, dead. Alf. Frank. Laurence. All long gone. The extraordinary names: Tom Tooth; Teresa Bone; Lionel Krimholz. So-and-so who committed suicide – 'She was so beautiful.' So-and-so who ran off with his wife's sister – 'They never spoke again.' So-and-so who always had an eye for my mum but who never made his move – 'Shame, really.' Out of about a hundred people, maybe just half a dozen are still alive. 'You know, we are very lucky really,' says my mum. My father proposes a toast to absent friends.

Stories we've heard a million times. The ten-bob dinner in the hall. The letter from my mum's boss: 'Dear Eileen, I have received your letter notifying us that you are to be married and asking permission that you might continue in employment.' The telegrams. My dad's Uncle Ted getting the bus in from Watford with Aunt Doll and the cousins. The three-day honeymoon in Cornwall with Fred and Ida. How my grandmother made all the wedding outfits – my mum's dress, the bridesmaids' outfits, her own outfit, my other grandmother's outfit. The argument about the bridesmaids, my grandmother insisting that they should both be the same height and size, so that they matched, 'for the photos'. How the lorry drivers at the depot did the music – the George King Trio, with George on vocals and piano, Dobbo on banjo and the other bloke whose name no-one can remember on drums. How George used to black-up to sing Al Jolson. Names matched to faces. Jew. Jew. Gypsy. Irish. Christian. Boxer. Seamstress. Cousin. Cousin. Navy. Marines. Whitechapel. Clerkenwell. Bethnal Green. Another world.

In the end we had beef brisket – terribly overcooked – and it was all over by 7.30 p.m., so my mum could get inside and watch her programmes.

Plenty of cake left over.

Saturday 29 August

My mum has always insisted on good manners at the table – no elbows, always a placemat, that sort of thing – but my dad finds it hard to remember the rules now. He starts eating as soon as he sits down at the table.

'It's because of the war,' says my mum, indulgently. 'And the Marines.'

I have made what turns out to be quite a rich dish of meatballs. My mum is up half the night and sick all day. I'm terrified. I lay awake all night. After all this, will it be the meatballs that kill my mum?

Monday 7 September

Have started new job. Most teaching is now online but I'm last in, so I'm going to be doing the face-to-face: masks, desks two metres apart, sanitizing stations.

Meet a new colleague – the only other one on campus. He attempts to do an elbow bump, while I do a *namaste* gesture. Embarrassing for both of us.

Saturday 26 September

'What's your recipe for whiskey cake?' I ask my mum.

'Wouldn't you like to know,' she says.

She still likes to make a cake once a week, at the weekend. Fruit cakes, mostly. It's a tradition. And my dad always likes to butter a slice of the cake – just to top up the calories.

'Ted!' says my mum. 'Ted!'

Sunday 27 September

Out in the country here, every morning there are two little fat birds that waddle up to the patio and then waddle away again. My ignorance when it comes to birds is never-ending.

'What are those little fat birds?' I ask my dad.

'Those?' says my dad. 'You don't know what they are?' It's one of his favourite ways of answering a question, with another question. He likes to catch me out. It amuses him. 'With all that education? OK. Here's your starter for ten. Who wrote *Paradise Lost*?'

'John Milton.'

'Ah well, all that education didn't go to waste then.'

How he knows that Milton wrote *Paradise Lost* I have no idea. I've never seen him read a book. It was probably on *The Chase*.

'They're partridges,' says my mum.

Saturday 3 October

Went to my mum and dad's local butchers – had never been there before. (They prefer what they call 'supermarket meat'.) I walk in, mask on, scarf, my long beard poking through the bottom, my sort of beanie hat on – and the butcher and a customer are complaining loudly about 'bloody Pakis' not sticking to the rules. When they turn around and see me I can see them note the beard and the hat, and the fact that I'm not a local – and they stop talking.

Monday 5 October

A dream last night in which Ursula K. Le Guin was comforting me – I said I couldn't write. She said, fine, just take a break and return refreshed.

Relentless rain for days – unceasing. Leak in the garage roof.

Last week: daughter's friend's dad died suddenly; younger son broke up with Spanish girlfriend; my dad had blood in his urine (again), arranged appointment with doctor.

Things in China are more or less back to normal, apparently.

Wednesday 7 October

I am teaching in a converted drama studio: no windows, markings on the floor. A special ventilation system has been installed. I wear a visor, the students are in masks. It feels like being in a 1970s Soviet sci-fi film.

'You said that last week,' says a student.

Saturday 10 October

'What are these?' says my dad. I've made a fish dish, which I have sort of garnished – gestured at – with capers.

'They're capers,' I say.

'What are they when they're at home?' he asks.

I have no idea. I look it up. Capers are the small flower buds of the *Capparis* shrub that grows in the Mediterranean. They're picked by hand, which is why a tiny jar is so expensive. A corner-shop find – next to the jars of cockles.

Friday 6 November

'What do you miss most?' I ask my mum.

'Costa,' she says, without hesitation.

I know what she means.

They love a Costa, the pair of them. They used to drive up to the one at Tesco. They like it milky – the atmosphere, as much as the coffee.

I used to write in cafes, in the old days – the brilliantly misnamed Cafe

Brazilia mostly, back home in NI, until it closed just before the first lock-down, after more than twenty years of trading.

I wrote my first five books in Cafe Brazilia. I would gather up the children in the morning, then drop off one or two and eventually three to nursery or to school, and then hurry to Brazilia for a couple of hours before the necessary round of pick-ups began. At home there were always other things to do: the washing, the tidying, the cleaning. Brazilia was my workplace. I'd always order a filter coffee – which came in two strengths, Strong or Medium, and two sizes, Regular or Large. I was always Regular, Strong. The children used to love the pancakes with maple syrup. At one time I knew most of the staff by name. One year I was there so much, we exchanged Christmas cards and presents.

It was nothing special, Cafe Brazilia. It was ordinary. Which is why it was so good.

Saturday 7 November

I go into my parents' kitchen while they're napping in the afternoon. I'm wearing plastic gloves and a face mask. I'm looking for a jar of paprika for tonight's dinner. My mum has three jars of paprika – all bought by me. They should see us through. I like a bit of paprika – even my dad likes paprika, my paprika chicken – but when I'm cooking paprika chicken I am always reminded of some lines by John Berryman, in *The Dream Songs*: 'Filling her compact & delicious body / with chicken paprika'. I hate those lines. Poets ruin everything.

Tuesday 17 November

I'm in a taxi. I haven't been in a taxi in six months or more.

How's Covid been for you, I ask.

He had it back in March. He recovered. But he now has 'sticky blood'. Then his brother-in-law got it and died, and then his sister too. He's lost all his contract work. I regret having asked.

'Not good then,' I say.

'Not good,' he agrees.

Sunday 13 December

Again and again, going into my parents' house when they are asleep or dozing, masked, gloves on – to cook or clean.

My mum has a sugar cupboard – a cupboard just for sugar. She always has granulated sugar, caster sugar, golden caster sugar, icing sugar, light brown sugar and dark brown sugar. When we were young my dad would regularly make three meals: toast for breakfast during the week, a fried breakfast at the weekends, and sugar sandwiches for snacks. White sliced bread, butter, sugar. With a cup of tea, two sugars. We had them as a treat when watching telly.

I have had a toothache for about a month. No dentist here will see me.

Thursday 24 December

My wife and I are up at 5.30 a.m. in the garage, as usual. My wife likes to exercise. I like to read. Heavy rain outside. It has been raining for days – weeks. By 7 a.m. we are sitting quietly drinking coffee when we notice there are swans in the garden – swans! – and that the garden is underwater. I rush out to the shed – everything's in the shed, all my work – and start hauling stuff into the garage. Notebooks, papers, books. Then I realize that the water is advancing towards the garage, rising about an inch every half hour. Then it starts coming in waves. The river has burst its banks.

By noon, the shed – which is nearest to the river – is a foot underwater. By late afternoon we are wading waist-deep. Cars are floating down the street. The garage is about to be flooded. My parents are safely upstairs in the house. Brian next door has been rescued by his son-in-law in a tractor.

Who do you call when there's a catastrophic flash flood? There is no one to call.

We waded through freezing cold water for about ten hours, shifting stuff. My mum and dad's next-door neighbour's bungalow completely underwater. The cottages next door all underwater. My mum and dad's house is a few feet higher and further from the river. Water is lapping at the back door.

As we're going to bed at 11 p.m., my mum stands on the stairs in her mask and says, 'Does that mean you're not cooking Christmas dinner tomorrow?'

Go to bed in the back room downstairs, wearing my clothes, just in case. The house is an island, completely surrounded by floodwater.

Friday 25 December

I get up at 5 a.m. Have barely slept. Set my alarm to wake me every hour. House still dry. Water receding. I wade out to the garage. It could be worse: the water has only just got in, and beneath the tiles it's a solid concrete floor – as befits a garage. I have never been so glad to be living in a garage.

I put on my wellies and start peeling brussels sprouts.

All the septic tanks have overflowed. The smell is bad. Rats.

An electrician called Andy arrives around 11 a.m. He's a friend of the son of the man who lives in the end cottage. He does a temporary fix on the electrics. By lunchtime we have the electricity back on. I ask him how much. He says he won't accept money from anyone on Christmas Day in circumstances like this. I make him take £50 in cash – which is all I've got – and give him a damp bottle of wine.

Friday 1 January 2021

Oh, yes, almost forgot: to the masked gang who broke into our younger son's house in Birmingham and smashed everything up and took everything: to hell with you, the lot of you. After the year we've all had, as a finale, that's the best you can do? You're kidding, right?

Windmills

DEAN FEE

It was almost completely dark when we pulled into the gravelled driveway. The headlights of the car illuminated trees and hedges before abandoning them again to darkness. The cottage had whitewashed walls with a low red door flanked by tiny wood-framed windows. My father rolled the car across the crunching gravel, pulled up alongside a small two-door car, flicked the remainder of his second cigarette out the window. If my mother were there, he would not have been smoking around me. I was a weak child and, amongst many other problems, I had a bad heart.

Now, Malachy, you be good and quiet when we go in here, he said. Have you got your button with you?

I thought we were going to the windmills, I said.

My father's phone vibrated in his pocket. He pulled it out and eyed it, reading, and after a moment said, The windmills?

I hummed a yes.

We'll see. I've this wee job to do first. Now, have you got your button?

I rubbed the lump in my pocket and nodded. It was a school night and after everything that had happened recently, I knew I was lucky to be out so late.

I'll be good, I said.

Right, come on then, my father said, unbuckling his seatbelt.

I did the same and pulled my sleeves down over my hands and waited for him to open his door and step out. It was cold out there by the sea and my teeth immediately started to chatter. I shadowed my father's steps to the boot, from which he pulled out a rattling old toolbox, and we approached the door. He rapped it with his knuckles and we stood back to wait.

The door opened an inch before getting stuck, and then was tugged to open fully. There was a woman standing in flickering candlelight. Her hair was starkly black against her stained white frock, and she was holding a mobile phone to her chest. I could not tell her age but I knew she was older than my father. There was the wet and warm stink of an animal.

Simon, she said. Sorry I was late getting back.

Her eyes were black.

Ah not a bother, Joyce, my father said, and ducked his lanky frame into the building. I followed him in and Joyce closed the door after me.

And who's this? she said.

This is my boy, Malachy. Say hello, Mal.

I greeted the bare concrete floor with a muffled hello.

Isn't he a handsome boy? she said. Just like his father.

She thumbed the beads of her necklace and brought them to her mouth as though she wanted to chew them.

It's just through on the right, she said, pointing, but my father was already turning the cast-iron doorknob. There was a high-pitched keening, an animal sound, and another wave of the smell, stronger this time.

I'm so glad you came, said Joyce. Massimo won't stop crying and keeps chewing on his cage and escaping. Do you hear him? He's constantly at it. Always crying about something and digging at his straw.

I could hear a scratching sound now, along with the keening.

The floor was covered in newspaper. The walls were whitewashed, like the outside of the cottage, and covered in A4-sized pictures of religious figures. There were multiple shots of Pope John Paul II cut from magazines – blessing and genuflecting and kissing the heads of babies – as well as formal portraits not only of him but of his predecessors, all mixed together with black and white images of Elvis Presley and Johnny Cash and one lone postcard-sized image of Bruce Lee in an action pose.

The only chair in the room was covered with a patchwork quilt depicting

biblical scenes. I recognized St Sebastian feathered with arrows and a blood-
ied Jesus burdened by his cross. There was a fold-up table set beside it, on
which sat a lone cup half full of milky tea. A three-legged table in the corner
held two red candles that cast flickering shadows on an oval frame bearing
the image of a tanned and bearded man.

The only other thing in the room was the source of the noise and smell.
On the floor, in a large hutch made of a light timber frame and chicken-wire
mesh, pale yellow straw had been laid down to create a bed. I stepped
towards it for a better look, and something in the far corner of the hutch
began to rustle and whine.

Do you see there where he has the mesh chewed away, Simon?

Aye, my father said. In the corner there.

Joyce had blocked up the hole using a stack of red bricks.

Do you think you can fix it? she said. I have a roll of mesh out in the shed.

He nodded and said he could do it, no problem.

Oh that's brilliant, she said. Between him squealing and the noise of these
windmills they've put up on the hill, my head is pounding. Can you believe
the hospital in town doesn't have an A&E anymore? I had to drive all the way
out to Our Lady of Mercy's to be seen for my headaches.

Aye, it's dreadful, my father said. Sure weren't we only out there the
other night with this lad.

Oh God, she said, turning to me. Are you all right, pet?

I avoided her eyes.

He's grand, my father said. He's prone to taking dwams. Wee fainting fits.
It wasn't so bad when we had the hospital here fully functioning, but now
we have to boot it the half hour down the road. The missus does be in an
awful state.

That's horrible, Simon. How is Olivia anyway?

Not a bother on her, he said. Speaking of, we'll have to get this boy home
ASAP. She'll be worried.

Of course, she said.

We're on high alert now, though. Isn't that right, Mal? Show Joyce what you have for when you don't feel well.

I didn't budge, and my father told Joyce that I was shy. Come on, Mal, show us your wee beeper.

After a moment I took the black plastic oval from my pocket and proffered it to the adults. There was a red button countersunk in the centre of it.

Go on and press it, Mal. Wait'll you hear this, Joyce.

I complied, feeling the button click beneath my thumb, and the room was filled with the electronic wail of two resonating notes bouncing off each other, like the siren of an ambulance. The guinea pig squealed in discordant harmony.

Off! Off! my father shouted, laughing.

Joyce had her hands over her ears, and left them there for a few moments after the noise dissipated.

That's some racket it makes, she said.

It's worth it for peace of mind alone, my father said. Any time Mal feels even a slight bit unwell he can hit that button and I'll come running.

I smiled up at him and he returned it with a wink.

Right, I'll get this mesh, he said.

I went to follow him, but he told me to wait. Have a look at the guinea pig, my father said. Joyce, you'd hardly make us a cup of coffee? I've been up since early with work and I'm bolloxed.

Oh, of course, she said, and they both left the room. I watched the door swish open and closed, catching a brief glimpse of the kitchen, of its blue cabinets and its floor also layered in old newspapers.

Left alone in the room, I turned my attention back to the hutch. I hunkered down, resting my hand on its roof, and made sucking noises through my teeth to entice the animal out of its cover. The straw rustled again and fell away to show Massimo's little blond head. He sniffed the air and made a squeaking noise that sounded like a dog's chew toy. I stuck a finger through the chicken wire, wiggled it and echoed the animal's squeaks, but I was ignored. Massimo put his head back under the straw and lay there shivering.

On the corner table beside the picture of the bearded man was an old sepia mass card. It was long, like a bookmark, and on it was written: In Loving Memory of Massimo Rossi, Beloved Son and Devoted Husband.

I heard the shudder of the back door closing and the swish of my father's feet being wiped on the inside mat before he re-entered the room with the roll of mesh gripped in one hand.

Poor wee prick is having a bad time, isn't he? he said.

I asked who and he nodded towards the hutch and said, Massimo here.

He's lonely, I said.

My father looked up and me and said, Yeah?

Yeah, guinea pigs aren't supposed to be on their own. They don't like to be alone. That's why he's crying and trying to get out all the time.

Jaysus, I didn't know that.

Joyce backed herself into the room with a rattling tray of cups, a pot and a plate of biscuits. She spoke her own actions out loud as she did them, placing the tray on the chair and transferring the contents to the fold-up table, lilting on about which cup was for who and listing out the assortment of biscuits.

Would you like a wee biscuit, Malachy?

I said no thank you.

He does, my father said. He's just being polite. Go on and take one, son.

I conceded and took a foiled Viscount. They were expensive and my mother never bought them. Joyce insisted I take another one, saying they were only small. I took a chocolate finger instead and I ate it straight away as it had already started melting in my hand. I put the Viscount in my pocket.

Massimo had shoved himself into the furthest corner of his hutch, to get away from my father's hands and the snips he was using to clear away the chewed wire.

Joyce tried to hand my father his coffee, but he told her he'd get it in a minute. A silence fell on the room as Joyce and I watched him work. He rolled out the chicken wire and clipped a square out of it with the snips. He popped his toolbox open and the lid fell back to reveal many smaller compartments. It was like a magic trick. My father pulled out a hammer and a spiky handful of tiny U-nails and called me over to hold the wire in place while he tacked it to the timber frame.

Mal says Massimo is lonely, my father said.

Joyce made a questioning noise.

Yeah, my father said, beginning his tapping. He says guinea pigs aren't supposed to be on their own. Says they get lonely and that's why he's acting out.

Is that right? said Joyce, turning her attention to me. Where did you hear that, Malachy?

I didn't like her gaze on me and kept my focus on holding the mesh and muttered my answer.

I read it in a book I got for Christmas, I said.

Aren't you a clever boy? Did your Daddy get you that book?

No, my Mammy did.

There was a silence before I went on, It's actually illegal to have only one guinea pig in Switzerland. It's seen as an act of cruelty.

Joyce's gaze sidled from me to her tea and she ringed the rim of the cup with an idle finger. My father grunted to his feet and dusted his hands and told Joyce that I always had my nose in a book.

He's a regular bookworm, he said, looking down at me with smiling admiration. Let's hope he makes something of it so he can look after me when I get older. I don't want to be penniless all my life.

He chuckled to himself and then told Joyce that that's that.

Oh, that's excellent, she said. Hopefully that'll keep him locked in. I had to put newspaper down in all the rooms because he likes to wander when he gets out, shitting everywhere. Don't you, Massimo?

She walked over to the cage and bent down to address the guinea pig, who pointed his nose up at her expectantly. Her hands were clasped between her knees, causing her dress to ride up at the back. You'll never get away from me now, will you? No you won't.

When she stood erect again she let a hand fall loose to touch, for a brief moment, the inside of my father's wrist. He visibly straightened as if to get away, but she had already let go. She glided past him, turning her head to look him in the eye as she did so.

I caught his eyes and he cleared his throat.

Come on and get that tea into you, lad, and we'll get going. Your mother will kill me if I have you out too late, especially since you're only out of the hospital.

I looked down at the tea where I had left it on the floor beside the hutch. I had no interest in drinking it. It was too hot.

That reminds me, said Joyce. I have these for you, Malachy.

She reached into a discreet pocket waist-height on her dress and pulled out a foiled sleeve of tablets.

These are vitamins for you. They'll keep your strength up. Make your bones good and strong and keep your heart and head at an even keel.

I didn't immediately take the offered tablets. My father told me to not be rude, good lad.

I pocketed the crinkling package and thanked Joyce.

You're very welcome, young man, she said. I take them all the time and they keep me healthy.

My father took his coffee off the table, gave it a tentative sip before drinking half the cup in one gulp. He smacked his lips and exhaled and picked up the roll of chicken wire to return it to the shed.

Gather up those tools there, good lad. I'll be back in a minute.

Joyce followed him out the door, thanking him again for the job. I knelt beside the toolbox and flexed the lid to watch the compartments move within. I sucked my teeth at Massimo again, who had scrambled across to see if his escape hole was still there. He sniffed at the new mesh, poking his nose out so that I could touch it if I wanted, but I was wary of his big front teeth.

The back door closed again and I could hear the two adults talking in a low rumble. I put the hammer and the unused nails into the box with a clatter that drowned out their conversation, but when the room fell silent again I heard my father say, That's way too much money, Joyce. It was only a small job.

It's not just for the hutch, said Joyce.

I can't take it, Joyce. I have to go. The boy's not well, I can't leave him on his own for long.

It won't be long, Simy. It'll only take a minute.

There was the crinkle of paper money and Joyce said something about hospital bills. Her voice was heavy, like she was out of breath, and I wondered how long before I'd be able to get home if my father had another job to do. I didn't like this house and I wanted to go see the windmills.

I let the lid fall closed with a clang that sent Massimo scampering through his straw to bury his head once again. The tea had cooled a little and so I lifted it and took a sip, wanting it to taste like adulthood. There were still biscuits left on the plate, so I took another chocolate finger and ate it quickly, worrying that Joyce would notice the deficit or that my father would smell the new chocolate on my breath. I took another sup of tea to wash it down and as I was swirling it around in my mouth my father came back into the room holding his car keys.

Here, son, he said, holding them out. Are you strong enough to carry that toolbox out to the car for me?

I nodded, my guilty mouth paused in its chewing. I reached out and took the heavy bunch of keys.

That's the car key there, with the big M on it. Just put it in my door and turn it right. There's a lever down on the right-hand side under the steering wheel. Give that a good pull and it'll open the boot. Don't be afraid to pull it hard, it won't break.

I swallowed and said I would.

You're a good boy. I've just another wee job to do here and I'll be out to you. You can read while you wait. All right?

Okay, Daddy, I said, and placed the cup back on the floor and moved over to the toolbox, locked the latch and grabbed the handle with both hands and hefted it so it swung between my legs. My father smiled sadly and disappeared again behind the door and closed it tight.

Outside, full night had come. There was no breeze. I shuffled my way round to the driver's side between the two cars. I eased the toolbox to the gravel with a crunch and looked in the window of Joyce's car. There were newspapers and large books and scattered beauty products: a long sunburst comb, the spiky cylinder of a hairbrush missing its handle, a small blue and white tub that said Hand Cream, and an eyelash curler with its crosshatch shadow thrown behind it by the moon.

Turning away, I fumbled for the keys, located the fat one with the big M on it and slotted it into its hole and turned. I pulled the door open with care to avoid Joyce's car and bent down to paw in the dark for the boot's lever. It smelled like dirt and rubber and stale smoke in the driver's seat hollow. I found the lever, hooked my fingers around it and pulled it towards myself with a clunk. Behind me I heard the pop of the boot opening. Once I hauled the box in, I pushed it in with a heave and closed the boot. The window to the left of the front door was now lit with a buttery swaying light, its curtains closed. I looked down the lane towards the lapping bay and watched the moonlight reflected in a jagged line across the water. It looked like a pathway.

The inside of the car was stuffy with dust and I was forced to breathe through my mouth. The windows would only go down if I turned the ignition on. That was a no-go, so I sat stifled. I tried to turn the overhead light on so I could read, but the button wouldn't work. I settled back into my seat and looked out the window. The cottage was a dark outline through the grimy windscreen and my eyes were trained on the door, expecting it to open any minute. I willed it to open, to give me my father back so I could go home. I wondered would my mother still be up watching TV or would she have gone to bed. It was well past my own bedtime by now. I pictured the journey back home: how the boats in the harbour would look in the dark, tall black masts reaching up to the sky.

The moon had dipped behind the clouds and a wind had picked up, giving the trees a dark bluster that unsettled me. I ran my thumb along the circle of the button in my pocket, wanting to press it, but instead I turned my focus back to the car. I spotted the yellow box of my father's matches and picked them up with a quick shake like he always did. I slid the drawer out with a finger and pinched one of the red-topped sticks out. Closing the drawer, I gripped it between thumb and forefinger and – to test – slowly grated the tip along the bumped edge of the box. Nothing happened, so I did it again, quickly this time, and the match flared into life. There was a split second of chaos before it settled into a familiar flame and illuminated my surroundings. I held it before my eyes and let it burn down, curling the match black, until it got too hot for my fingers. I blew it out then and, in the darkness, inhaled the sulphuric smoke, relishing the taste.

It was a while before the light from the door opening caught my eye and I watched my father settle his coat on. Joyce stood in the doorway beside him, a hand laid on his shoulder. I closed my eyes and pretended to be asleep. I could hear them say something but couldn't make it out and then the driver's door opened and he got in, his weight shifting the car on its axis.

Were you dozing, son? he said.

No, I said, purposefully short.

He pulled down his sun-visor and stuck something into its plastic band before starting the car. As he reversed he beeped the horn in a farewell salute. The headlights picked up the light rain that had started to fall. When we got to the bottom of the hill, he apologized for being so long.

You're not mad at me, are you?

I said I was. I said, You were gone for ages.

He lit a cigarette and rolled down the window.

It was a big job. It took longer than I expected. Were you scared? he said, teasing me and nudging my leg with a knuckle.

No, I said again.

Aw, was little Malachy scared?

Again I said I wasn't, shouting a little, which made him laugh.

The road straightened out and I looked out towards the sea but couldn't see it.

Alright, he said, shoving the cigarette into the corner of his mouth and putting both hands on the wheel. I'm sorry. I'll make it up to you. Do you want to go see the windmills?

I thought he was trying to trick me so I said nothing.

You don't want to go? That's fine. We can just head on home and go to bed.

No, I said at last. I want to go.

He laughed and I couldn't help but smile and asked would it not be too dark and he said it might be but we'll have a look anyway.

But you can't tell your mother. She'd only be worried.

I agreed to say nothing.

He took a right turn a few minutes later and we made our way up a winding hill road that forced my shoulders back into the seat, the lights of the car often disappearing into the night sky as we climbed. Eventually the windmills came into view. They looked out over the bay, pale sentinels of the foothills, their blades slowing rotating as though they alone powered the earth.

As we crept closer my father told me that the boxes at the back that balance their propellers were about the size of a small car.

You wouldn't think it from down here, he said, but they are.

When we got close enough he angled the car so I could see them clearly through my window. I asked could we get out, but the rain was too heavy now and I was told no. Not with my chest. So we sat in the idling car, with the window rolled down to look, spits of rain landing on my face.

Notes on contributors

MAGGIE ARMSTRONG is working on a novel.

NATHAN DUNNE is a freelance journalist and the author of *Lichtenstein*, a study of the painter's work. He is working on a collection of short stories.

DEAN FEE is working on a collection of short stories.

DAVID RALPH is an assistant professor of sociology at Trinity College Dublin.

IAN SANSOM's most recent book is *September 1, 1939: W.H. Auden and the Afterlife of a Poem*.

JESSICA TRAYNOR's most recent collection of poems is *The Quick*.